THE SECRET

Revealed

By

CJ Nash

**Grosvenor House
Publishing Limited**

This book is published by
Grosvenor House Publishing Ltd
Link House
140 The Broadway, Tolworth, Surrey, KT6 7HT.
www.grosvenorhousepublishing.co.uk

This book is a work of fiction. Any resemblance to
people or events, past or present, is purely coincidental.

A CIP record for this book
is available from the British Library

ISBN 978-1-80381-586-2
eBook ISBN 978-1-80381-587-9

Dedication

I dedicate
this book to my family. My Husband Steve,
my girls
Emily and Libbie, my Parents and Sister.
Thank you
for all your Love and support through
this journey
in writing my first book.

CHAPTER 1

Jazmin's Story

It was two days before my 18th birthday, and I was having another fight with my parents. I had wanted to go out as a family for dinner on Saturday to celebrate but, as usual, they were too busy. They were always busy where I was concerned; they were never around for any show I did, or birthday. I was lucky if they were even in to make dinner.

"Mum, I'm going to be 18. I just want to have a family dinner out. Is that really too much to ask?" Mum just looked at me.

"As you know, we are due to go to a fundraiser on Saturday, so yes, it is too much to ask."

"You're never around for me. Why did you even have me when you obviously couldn't give a shit about me, or what I do? Every event I have ever been involved in, you have done whatever you could to get out of it. Neither of you are ever around. Why do you hate me so much?" By the time I'd finished speaking, I was in floods of tears. I was going to have another rubbish birthday, I could tell. I went to bed that night, as I did every night, alone and sad.

The next few days were quiet as I had finished college and was just waiting for my results. Saturday arrived, and my best friend, Emma, took me out for the day. She knew what my parents were like and knew that they wouldn't be there for me. When we got back, my parents were in.

"So, are we going out for dinner, then?" I asked my mum.

"No, Jazmin, I've told you – we are busy," she replied.

"Well then, as I'm obviously not a daughter you want around, I won't be here when you get back, so you don't need to be put out by me any more." On that note, I turned around and headed to my room. Emma followed me up the stairs.

"What are you going to do?" she asked.

"I don't know, but I can't stay where I'm not wanted, and I'm obviously not wanted here."

"You can come and stay with me for a few days, while you get yourself sorted out."

"Thank you so much, I really appreciate that."

We started packing up my things and loading them into my car, with Mum and Dad just watching on. They headed out before I finished, without even a goodbye or, 'please don't leave'. This helped me to know that I was making the right decision. That night I sleep on Emma's bedroom floor, wondering what I was going to do. Sunday was quiet as both Emma and I were taking it easy. Around 4pm, Emma's Mum called up to us, asking us to come downstairs. In the living room stood two police officers. I looked at them, and then at Emma's mum. She asked me to sit down and then sat down next to me. "What's up?" I asked. "Jazmin, they have some news for you." The female police officer sat down beside me. "Jazmin, we have some bad news about your parents." "What do you mean by bad news about my parents?" I asked. "They were involved in an accident last night – with another car. I'm very sorry to say that neither of them survived." I looked at the police officer, not knowing what to say. My parents were dead. I just didn't know how to feel. As much as I hated them for ignoring me, I would never wish this on them in a million years. I ran upstairs, shut myself in the bathroom, and just sat there.

Over the next few days, I became very ill. So much so, that Emma's mum ended up calling an ambulance and I was taken to hospital. Test upon test were ran on me, but they couldn't find what the problem was, so they concluded that it was all due to the death of my parents and the stress and upset it had caused. Eventually, I started to improve.

One afternoon, I was sitting up in bed watching the news. The Presenters, were talking about whether people with 'abilities' should be registered. More and more people were found to have various abilities, and others were starting to get scared. I didn't know what to think about it so turned over. That's when I heard someone crying from the next bed. I got up and walked over to see what was wrong. There was a girl about my age, laying there in tears, holding her head.

"What's wrong? Can I help?" I asked.

"My head hurts so much, but they say nothing is wrong."

"That sounds like a similar issue to me – they don't know what's wrong with me, either." I take hold of her hand and close my eyes. The next thing I knew, my hand was getting really hot. I opened my eyes, and there was a warm light coming from where my hand was touching the other girl's. She saw this, and I pulled away.

"My headache has gone. What did you do?"

"I don't know," I said. "I was just thinking that I wish I could help, and that's when my hand started to warm up."

"Oh, my god, you're a healer. They're rare, from what I've heard."

"What's a healer?" (I had no idea what she was going on about.)

"They're very rare people who have the ability to heal others, and I think you are one of them."

"Please don't say anything to anyone."

"I won't."

"Thank you." After that I went back to my bed.

The next day, Emma's mum came to pick me up to take me back to their place. They helped me sort out the funerals for my parents, and even paid for them. It was hard, going through all of this, but at least I had Emma and her family, who were more like parents to me than my own parents had been. The funerals were held together at a local church and then they were cremated. I went back to the house after it was all over and stayed there until after I got my results.

I passed with flying colours, and managed to get a job in Pimlico for a marketing company called Hammonds Marketing. It was a junior position but it was a start. Emma also got a job there, so it was good to have my best friend around. I sold my parents' house and bought myself a studio flat in Wraysbury, which was near where I had lived before, and I have now lived there, happily, for the past five years.

I hadn't told anyone about my powers over the last five years, but I had been practicing whenever I could. Apparently, I could heal animals as well as humans. I did not dare to see if I could do anything else, as I didn't want anyone to find out about me. I hadn't even told Emma, which I should have, really. People with powers don't always get a good name for themselves, hence why I had kept my head down. I had, however, tried to explore my limits by healing my own wounds, and helping animals I found injured. I'd even helped some homeless people who lived under the arches near where I worked; all in a way so that they didn't realise what I had done. It was interesting how I seemed to know what was wrong even when I couldn't see anything obvious.

Chapter 2

Jazmin's First Encounter

It had been a long day in the office and I couldn't wait to get home. I'd been working on a new project to get ready for the release of a new clothing line. (I'm still at Hammond Marketing, and they're still in Pimlico.)

"Sarah, have you seen the storyboard for the filming tomorrow?" I asked.

Sarah walked around the corner of my desk and moved a file to one side.

"There it is," she said.

"Sorry, Sarah. I'm losing the plot, what with all these late nights. I'll be glad when this is all done."

"Not long now," Sarah replied. "Filming is tomorrow, and then editing. The presentation is next Friday, and then that's it."

I wasn't convinced, but I smiled at Sarah and agreed with her, anyway.

Just then, Mr Underwood walked in. Mr Underwood had been my boss for the last two years, and I didn't like him. I tried to avoid him as much as possible.

"Everyone, come here please, I have an announcement to make."

"He's leaving, I hope," I say to Sarah. Sarah chuckled.

"As many of you are aware, HM has been struggling against the larger companies to get business."

"Shit, are we out of a job?" Sarah asked.

"No, Sarah, you're not. We have been taken over," He replied.

"Who's bought us out, then?" we heard from the other side of the room. It's Emma, my best friend, and Mr Underwood's secretary.

"The Blake Corporation. Mr Blake and his colleagues will be here this afternoon. So, make this place more presentable." With that said, Mr Underwood turned to go back to his office, calling for Emma as he went.

"Oh, my god," is all I could say. Sarah just stands in front of me with her mouth wide open, shaking her head.

"I knew things weren't great," she said, "but I didn't realise they were that bad."

"Matthew, Harry – please start tidying up all those boxes. Sarah, can you help me get these clothes tidied away?" This was the last thing we needed with all the prep work we still had for the shoot tomorrow.

"What's the plan?" Sarah asked.

"We'll just get the worst sorted out and the rest will have to do for now."

We got the tidying done and carried on with finishing off the prep work. It was just coming up to 4pm and

I was telling my team to make sure no one worked late today as it would be an early start, when I heard my name being called.

I turned around to see Mr Underwood standing with a group of people. There was one though who stood out from the crowd. He must have been 6ft 4in, with short, dark, well-manicured hair. He had a strong jawline and tanned skin. He wore a tailored suit that yelled 'money'. I didn't know what to say; I couldn't take my eyes off him. Power and confidence just rolled off him, and I had never seen a more handsome man. I pulled myself together.

"Yes, Mr Underwood, how can I assist?"

"Jazmin, I would like to introduce you to Mr Blake from The Blake Corporation. Could you please go through what your team is presently working on?" he asked.

"Of course," I said. "Mr Blake, it's a pleasure to meet you." As I shake hands with this amazing specimen of a man, I feel something like a static charge running between us. It is like nothing I have ever felt before.

"The pleasure is all mine and please, call me Justin," he replied.

I introduce Justin to my team, and go through the projects we have been working on and what we are doing at the moment. During that time, I constantly felt his eyes on me, as though there was no one else in the room. It made me feel uncomfortable and I kept squirming in my chair. *I'll be glad when it's time to hand him back over to Mr Underwood and go back to my work.* I handed Justin back to Mr Underwood, just before 5pm and headed back to my desk.

Emma sent me a quick Teams message about drinks after work. I wasn't planning on going, but I thought we had something – or should I say *someone* – to talk about.

CHAPTER 3

Justin's Anguish

How do I get myself into these things? Someone really has got to stop me from buying up these smaller firms. The only good thing about today was that woman Keith Underwood introduced me to. I have never seen green eyes like that before. They were like emeralds glinting in the sunlight. What was it about her?

I need to focus and decide what I'm going to do with HM. I was going to merge the business in with mine and get rid of the staff there, but after my conversation with Jazmin, I'm changing my mind...

"Marcus!" I shouted through my open office door. Marcus was my right-hand man – my PA. He made sure I got what I wanted, when I wanted, with whom I wanted. "There you are."

"Yes, Sir," he said.

"Find out everything you can on a Jazmin Cooper who works at Hammonds Marketing – personal, business – does she have a boyfriend? Everything and anything you can find."

"Yes, Mr Blake. How soon do you want this?" he asked.

"On my desk first thing."

"Yes, Sir."

Now that is out of the way, I should be able to focus on my work.

Justin spent the next two hours going through the report that his forensic accountant had put together on his new purchase. The more he read, the more convinced he was that someone was stealing from Hammonds Marketing. They had hidden it well, but not well enough. The hard bit was going to be figuring out who it was. With all the business that the company had, it didn't make sense for them to not be more cash-rich.

Looking at his watch, he realised that he was going to be late for the charity event he was due to go to tonight. (Another evening of being nice to all the bigwigs, trying to get him to support whatever new venture they had.) This was not going to be a good evening.

Suddenly, he found himself wondering what Jazmin was doing that evening, and whether she was on her own or not. Where the hell did that come from? *Why do I care what she's doing, or with whom?*

Justin got up from his desk, put his laptop and paperwork away, and walked to the lift. The good thing about owning the building was he had his own residence on the top floor. It made life so much easier.

As the lift doors opened onto the penthouse, Justin walked into the lavish living room. He looked out the floor-to-ceiling windows at the view over London. He loved that view and the peace it gave him. But he didn't have time to sit and relax now. He went to his bedroom and through to the large and spacious bathroom. He stripped and got in the very large shower. He only took a few minutes to freshen up before he got out to dry off. Justin's housekeeper had already arranged his dinner jacket on his bed, so he just needed to get dried off and dressed. It wasn't long, before he was done and back in the lift.

Chapter 4

Jazmin's Interesting Day

The day was finally at an end. I had reminded my team of where and when to meet for the filming, and then walked out the door with Emma. We walked across the street to our favourite watering hole. The Tavern was nothing special, but it suited our needs. It was quiet and unassuming; perfect for a catch-up.

"So, what was that with Justin?" Emma asked.

"What do you mean?"

"You were staring at one another as if there was no one else in the room."

"Emma, I don't know what you mean. Justin Blake is well out of my league, and I'm not exactly the type of woman he is known to go out with. He likes tall, thin, fake-breasted blondes with the personality of a broom cupboard. You've seen the photos of him at Gala's with the latest super model. Why on earth would he be looking at me?"

Emma just looked at me over her glass of wine and smiled.

"Stop that," I said. "How are things between you and Shawn, anyway?"

Shawn was Emma's new boyfriend, and they'd been seeing a lot of one another.

"Going well," she said. "The sex is amazing. He seems to know exactly what I need without me even saying anything."

"Good to know," I replied.

Emma has always been very open; not afraid to talk about anything. I, on the other hand, wouldn't say boo to a goose.

"So, you're going to carry on seeing him, then?" I asked.

"Yes. I don't know what it is, and I know it's only been a few months, but I think he may be the one."

"OMG, really? That's great. Just be careful though, please. You know you tend to jump head first into these things and then get hurt."

Emma had been about as successful with men as I had, which is not very.

"Anyway, time's getting on and I have an early start tomorrow, so I'm going to have to love you and leave you." Emma put on a sad face, but then gave me a big hug.

"Text me when you get home," Emma said.

"Yes, Mum," I replied.

Emma lived near the office, so didn't have far to go. My journey wasn't too bad – it was about an hour.

Once I got home, I dropped Emma a text and then took a quick shower. I made sure everything was ready for the morning and then had something to eat. I knew I would have to leave by 4.30am, so after eating, I went straight to bed.

That night, I had some rather saucy dreams about a very tall and handsome dark-haired man who I had met that day. I couldn't stop thinking about him, but I knew I needed to…

I awoke the next day feeling bereft, as if I was missing something. I pushed the feeling to one side and got ready. I was due to meet the team in Windsor Great Park, with the photographer and film crew. It was going to be a long day. At least it was Friday, so once we were done, that would be it for the weekend.

I arrived at the park just after 5.00am, as the sun was coming up. The sky was a beautiful mix of orange, red and yellow with a few wispy clouds. It would make a great backdrop. It was June, and it was perfect weather.

I set about ensuring everything was in place, and filming started around 7am. By 1pm, we had done a lot of the work, so we all took a break. As I was sitting in the shade, eating my pasta, a shadow came over me. I looked up and there, in front of me, was Justin Blake.

"Mr Blake, what are you doing here?" I asked.

"One: it's Justin," he said, "and two: this is a public park, so anyone can walk around here."

"True," I replied. I stood up and put my lunch away. "Well, as you're here, would you like to see how things have gone?"

"That's really why I'm here," he said.

Just what I need: the new owner pocking his nose around in my work. God, I feel so uncomfortable. The memory of my dreams last night kept coming back into my head. All the places he had kissed me and caressed me just wouldn't stop popping up. This was not going to be a fun afternoon.

I went through the plan for the shoot and how far we were into it. He came up with some good suggestions on some different camera angles, which worked really well. He then left me to it.

Things were going great. I was just adjusting an outfit on one of the models when I felt someone watching me. I looked up to see Justin's piercing blue eyes watching me from across the park. What was it about him? I needed to focus on what I was doing, and the fact that he kept watching me didn't help. The next thing I knew, Justin was standing in front of me.

"Off you go, Tia," I said to the model. She walked off to carry on with the filming.

"What are your plans for after the filming?" Justin asked me.

"To go home, and curl up with a glass of wine and a good book," I replied.

"What about food?" he asked.

"I'll probably just throw something together when I get home. Why?" He stared down at me, with a smile on his face.

"Well, when you're finished, you and I are going out for dinner."

"What? No. I can't," I replied.

"Why not?" Justin asked.

"I don't date people I work with. It just gets too complicated when it ends." I turned around, and carried on sorting things out.

We finished about 7.30pm. Everything got packed away and people started to head off. I hadn't seen Justin for a while, so I assumed he had already left. I was just about to head off when there was a tap on my shoulder.

"Have you forgotten about dinner?"

"Wow, you made me jump," I said.

"Sorry," he replied.

"Don't you remember that I said no?" I asked.

"Yes, but I don't take no for an answer."

"Oh, really?" I said. "Well, consider this the first time, then." I stood there, wondering what else he wouldn't accept no for. "Justin, I'm flattered, but it's been a long week and a very long day. I really just want to go home."

"That's fine, we'll get take out, then," he replied.

There really didn't appear to be any getting out of this.

"Fine then, but I chose what we eat."

"Fine by me," he replied.

We walked down the path to the car park at the bottom of the park, and there was a brand new Mercedes SUV, with a gentleman opening the back door.

"After you, Jazmin," Justin said as he guided me to the back of the car. I smiled and thanked the driver as I got in. Justin walked around to the other side and then got in. The driver then did the same, at which point Justin told him to drive to my place. It took me almost the full journey home, before I realised that I had not told them where I lived.

"Hold on: how do you know where I live?"

"Not now…"

"Justin, how do you know where I live?" I said more forcefully this time.

"We'll talk later," was all he said. I wasn't impressed with his answer, but I decided to leave it for now.

"Fine."

We pulled up outside my block of flats. It wasn't anything posh, but it did me fine. Justin got out first and walked around to open the car door for me. I stepped out, thanking the driver, and walked towards the main door. Once we were inside, Justin followed me up the stairs to the first floor and along the hall to my front door.

"It's not much, but it's home. Probably nothing like you're used to," I said.

"I'm not here to judge your home, I'm here to spend time with you."

I put the key in the lock and pushed the door open. I flicked the switch and the lights came on, then I walked in, with Justin following close behind. Before I knew what was happening, the front door had been closed and I'd been pushed up against it. I looked into Justin's eyes and saw – I don't know what – lust, maybe. I was not sure, really. He was using his body to hold me in place, while his left hand was against the door by my head. His right hand was stroking my cheek.

I continued looking up into his deep blue eyes, trying to work out what was happening. My breath caught as he moved closer. Our lips were almost touching, when he said to me:

"I've been wanting to do this from the minute I saw you."

"Why?" I ask.

"Shh."

Our lips touched and it was heavenly. He was gentle to start with, using his tongue to encourage me to open my mouth. Before I even realised what I was doing, my arms were around his neck, deepening our kiss. I felt as though sparks were flying between us; our tongues fighting for control. Justin tilted my head a little more to deepen the kiss further.

That was when I started to think again: *what am I doing?* I put my hands on his firm chest and pushed him away. "Justin, we hardly know each other," I said while trying to catch my breath.

"I know enough to know that I want you."

"Well, you can't always have what you want." I stepped away and asked him if he would like a drink.

"What do you have?"

"White wine, gin, vodka, juice, or water. Or I can make you a cup of tea or coffee." I tried to keep my distance, but he kept stepping closer.

"I want to lap you up while you scream out my name."

"Well, that's not available," I replied.

"Shame. I'll just have the wine for now, then."

I hurried around, sorting out glasses and getting the wine out of the fridge. I also grabbed a few takeaway menus and dropped them on the counter. "What food would you prefer?" I asked Justin.

"It's your choice. I like most foods."

I decided on Chinese, and chose my favourite of mushroom rice and chicken with ginger and spring onion. Justin chose shredded beef, and we got prawn crackers as well. The food didn't take long to arrive, and we decided to sit on the floor with the food on my coffee table.

"So, Justin, now you can answer my questions."

"And what questions would they be?"

"For a start, how did your driver know where I lived?"

"I told him earlier," he replied.

"And how did *you* know where I lived?"

"I have access to your file, so I looked it up." I stared at him, pondering his words.

"OK, then, why? You are usually seen with models and actors that are tall and blonde with big tits. I may be tall but the rest isn't me, so I say again, why me?" I was sitting in front of Justin, legs crossed, giving him a hard stare. I wanted answers as this didn't make sense to me. He sat there staring at me with a smile on his face.

"There's something about you that just pulls me in. Your eyes are stunning, and you have the most kissable lips that I have ever seen. The short time I've spent with you, I see how caring and thoughtful you are. To me, you are beautiful and amazing, and I want to get to know you better."

I could feel my face getting red as no one had ever said anything like that to me before. I didn't know how to reply; I was shocked. Justin then got up and started to clear away our rubbish.

"Where does all this need to go?" he asked.

"Hold on, you can't say something like that and then act as though nothing has changed. I've known you for all of 24 hours."

"You're right, it has only been 24 hours, but I know what I want when I see it, and I want you, so you're mine and no one else."

"That's very presumptuous of you."

"Just stating a fact."

"And what if I don't want to date you?"

"I can be very persuasive when I want to be."

"I bet you can." I looked at Justin and shook my head. "Well, on that note, it's late and I need some sleep."

"Are you throwing me out?" asked Justin.

"Yes, I am. So off you go. I'll see you when you're next in the office, I'm sure."

"I'm sure you will, but as I'm not due in until next Friday, I'll be seeing you tomorrow." After that comment, he gave me a chaste kiss and walked out the door.

Chapter 5

Jazmin's Day Out

I stood there looking at the space he had only just occupied, with my mouth wide open. The cheek of it. Who did he think he was? I headed into my bathroom and cleaned my teeth, ready for bed. I still couldn't quite believe what had happened that evening.

As I live in a studio flat, my bedroom was in the main room. It was on a raised area, past my living room. As I got into bed, my phone bleeped. I checked the message, and it was from him. *But I didn't give him my number*, I thought to myself. The text read: *sleep well, my sweet. See you at 11am*. OMG, what next? I was going to make sure I was out. I knew it was a little childish but I was not having him boss me around. I didn't respond, and just put my phone on silent. As it was, I happened to be meeting Margaret from work tomorrow. She had asked me to help her find an outfit for a wedding she was going to in a few weeks.

All night I dreamt of Justin; the kiss we shared, and what I'd like him to do to me. By the time I got up,

I hadn't had much sleep. I typed two text messages: one to Margaret confirming the time and place to meet, and one to Justin saying I was not free that weekend. After that, I showered, dressed, had something to eat, and headed out the door.

I had a great day out with Margaret. We found her a beautiful pale pink outfit to wear, and had a lovely lunch in a little bistro near London Bridge. I hadn't looked at my phone all day, but I was still surprised to see two missed calls and four text messages – all from Justin.

I got in, put my bags down and plonked myself on the sofa. I was just about to answer my texts, when there was a knock at the door. *For pity's sake, I've just sat down.* I was just getting up when the person started banging on my door. "I'm coming!" I shouted. I looked through the peephole and saw Justin standing at the door looking rather angry. I opened the door and all I get from him is:

"Where have you been?"

"Out," I said. "What's it to you?"

"I've been trying to get hold of you all day."

"And I messaged you this morning, saying that I'm busy all weekend."

Justin walked past me and I slammed the door behind him.

"I've been worried sick."

"Well, as you can see, I'm fine. I told you I'd see you next time you're in the office."

"And I told you, you're mine, and I'd see you before then." I took a deep breath and tried to calm myself down.

"I'm sorry if you've been worried, but we've had one kiss. A relationship that does not make." Justin gave me a funny look, then walked right up to me, held my hands and says:

"You're mine," and then kissed me as no one had ever kissed me before. He then dropped one of my hands and started to caress my flushed cheek, encouraging me to open more for him. His other hand started to work its way up my arm, stroking as he went. He then started to tweak my nipple, making me gasp with pleasure. I put my hands on his chest; felt his tight abs under his shirt. While playing with my nipple, he moved his hand from my face and clasped my behind, to pull me into him. I could feel his thick shaft, pressing against my stomach. *Oh, my god, he's big. I'm already wet for him. I've known this man for five minutes and I'm reacting this way, already.* This was too much. I suddenly stopped the kiss and pushed him away.

"Sorry, Justin, but I can't just jump into bed with you. That's not who I am."

Justin looked at me as he tried to calm himself down. He leaned his forehead against mine and then gave me a warm hug.

"OK. Can I take you out to dinner tomorrow?"

"OK, but not too late as I'm sure my boss won't be happy if I'm late for work on Monday."

"Don't worry about him, but that's not a problem. I'll pick you up at 5pm so we can eat and be back early. How's that sound?" I looked at him and smiled.

"That would be perfect, thank you."

Justin took my hand and held it while we walked to the door. He kissed it and then gave me a gentle kiss on the lips.

"Till tomorrow," I replied, and he left. I shut the door and leaned against it. Touching my lips, which were still a little swollen, I smiled. *Can this really be happening to me? I just can't believe it.*

I texted Emma to ask if she was free for a chat. I put that it was about Justin, hoping that would push her along. Within five minutes, she was on the phone, and I told her everything that had happened since he had turned up at the shoot on Friday.

"Oh, my god, Jaz, that's amazing. You are so in there. You should ask for a pay rise. Have you done the deed yet? What's he like?"

"Emma, no, we haven't, and no, I'm not asking for a raise. I barely know him, and we've only kissed."

"OK, so what was it like?" she asked.

"Amazing. God, it was good. It does make me wonder what else he can do with his tongue." Emma laughed down the phone.

"You know, I'm not going to be able to look at him in the same way, now."

"How do you think I feel, Ems? I'm the one who's had his tongue down my throat!"

We carried on chatting for probably an hour, until Emma had to go to get ready for her date with Shawn. I then got on with my chores with a cheesy smile on my face. I slept well that night, and then got done everything I wanted to, out of the way, in time for when Justin arrived.

"So, where are we going?"

"You'll see," he said.

"I don't like surprises."

"I've noticed," he said.

He took me to a beautiful restaurant, and the food was to die for. He was a real gentleman, and didn't even try anything when he dropped me off home. I was kind of a little disappointed as he only gave me a peck on the cheek, but I smiled and let him go.

What a weekend I'd had.

CHAPTER 6
Justin's Intrigue

On Friday I walked into my office. Marcus had left the information I wanted on my desk; everything I could possibly want to know about Jazmin Cooper.

She was born and bred in Wraysbury, and lived there with her mother and father in a small house on the outskirts of the town. Tragedy struck on her 18th birthday when her mum and dad were killed in a car accident. Jazmin was left all alone to sort everything out, as she had no siblings. *Wow, she's been through a lot for such a young woman.* She ended up selling the house and buying her little studio flat, and has been living there ever since. Joined Hammonds Marketing straight out of college and worked her way up. No apparent boyfriend and not much of a social life. Salary could be better; good prospects. *Dealing with all that on her own must have been so hard. Well, I'm here for her now.*

"Marcus, find out where Jazmin Cooper is shooting today, and get me there." I made a note of her personal mobile number so I had it on me, and her home address. I was then out the door and in my car. Fred, my driver, got me to Windsor Park in no time, and that's where I saw her. She was sat under a tree, looking at some paperwork, eating her lunch.

When I saw her, I know there and then that she was mine. I just needed to convince her of that fact. There was just something about her that captivated me, and her eyes... The vibrancy of the colour was like nothing I'd seen before.

I walked up to her and stood there until she looked up. She called me Mr Blake again, so I had to remind her to call me Justin. I didn't want her to look at me and see the CEO of her company; I wanted her to see the man who was going to make her scream out my name in pleasure.

She went through the plan for the day and told me how things had been going. I made a few suggestions which went down well. I then stepped back and watched what was going on – mainly watching Jazmin, that was. I wondered what she was doing after this. After about an hour, I walked up to Jazmin.

"What are your plans for after filming?"

"To go home, curl up with a glass of wine and a good book, and rest."

I asked her about food. She said she would just throw something together.

Well, that's not going to happen, I thought to myself. "When you're finished here, I'm taking you out for dinner." She looked at me in shock and just said no, she didn't get involved with people from work. No one had ever said no to me before. She just turned around and carried on with what she was doing. I left her to it then, but that was not the end of that conversation.

For the next few hours I watched from the side-lines; went through my emails on my phone, and made a few calls. It was just coming up to 7.30pm when I saw everything being packed away. Jazmin was looking around but didn't see me. I walked up behind her and tapped her on the shoulder.

"Did you forget about our dinner date?" I made her jump. She then reminded me that she had said no. It was that word again. I was just not used to it.

"I won't take no for an answer," I said to her.

She still didn't budge. *What is it with this woman? God, I want to kiss those rosy, plump lips of hers.*

"I'm sorry, Mr – sorry, Justin – but it's been a very long day and I just want to go home."

"How about a takeaway at your place instead, then?"

She stood there contemplating my suggestion, and I could see the creases in her brow as she thought. *How I would love to smooth those away with my lips.* She finally agreed, and I took her hand and we walked down the path to the bottom car park. This was where Fred was waiting with the car. We got in and I told Fred to go to Jazmin's place. All of a sudden, she literarily shouts:

"Hold on! How do you know where I lived?"

"Not now, we'll talk later." I don't necessarily mean that, as I have other plans, but it stopped the questions. I had itched to touch her; more so since we got in the car. We got to her place quite quickly. It was a simple block of flats near the river, and the area was pleasant enough. We got out of the car and went to the main entrance, then walked through the door and headed up the stairs. *If I don't kiss her soon, I'm going to lose my shit.* Finally, we were at her front door. She let us in and I had her up against the door before she even had a chance to put her stuff down. Our lips were almost touching, when I say:

"I've been wanting to do this since the minute I saw you."

"Why?" she asked, but I didn't reply.

I kissed her – gently to start with – then coaxed her mouth open with my tongue. The kiss was nothing like I've had before. I could feel sparks shooting between us, like fireworks on New Year's Eve. Her arms slid around my neck and I deepened the kiss. This just made me want her even more. Before I knew it, though, she was pushing me away. She told me that we hardly knew each other. I wanted her, and I told her so, but again she is saying no to me, without saying the word. I was so not used to this.

She moved away from me and offered me a drink. I just wanted to lap her up, but accepted a wine. We ordered takeout and spent the evening chatting. She lacked self-confidence as she kept asking me why I wanted her. I thought it was because she considered herself to be overweight. She was just perfect to me, and I tell her again that she was mine, but now I was being presumptuous. She did make me smile, and that was one of the things I liked about her. This was going to be fun.

She then sent me home, telling me she would see me the next time I was in the office. I told her I'd see her tomorrow. I did love to watch her when I tried to wind her up. But I did have every intention of seeing her that weekend.

I got home, and text her straight away: *Sleep well, my sweet. I'll pick you up at 11am.* I sent the message and sat looking at my phone, waiting for a reply. Nothing came back. I ended up working for a few more hours, but by the time I got to bed, there was still no response. I was not happy, and unused to being ignored. All night long, I dreamt of all the things I'd love to do to Jazmin: eating ice cream off those amazing tits of hers; fucking her every which way I can. When I awoke, I found that I had had my first wet dream since I was a teenager and, since I was now 30, that had been a few years ago.

No woman had ever had this effect on me. I got up, took a cold shower, and checked my phone. She had finally responded but said she was busy. I tried to call her but got no response, so I sent her another text. Again, no response. Over the next several hours, I kept trying to get hold of her but to no avail.

I eventually got to the point where I was jumping into my car and heading to her home. I knocked on her door but there was no response. Now I was worried – really worried – and it was a feeling I was not used to; another new feeling for me.

I went and sat in my car, and waited. It got to 4pm, and I saw her walking along the road with a few bags in her hands. I was tempted to jump out and have words with her straightaway, but decided to give her a chance to get in. After about five minutes, I headed to her door and knocked. No response, so I started banging.

"I'm coming!" I hear from the other side. Jazmin opens up.

"Where have you been?"

"Out," she says. "What's it to you?" I couldn't believe what she had just said.

"I've been trying to get hold of you all day."

She reminded me that she did text to say she was busy that weekend. But I didn't care; I just wanted her. I walked in and shut the door behind me.

"I've been worried sick." *Does she not realise how much she means to me?* We bickered back and forth for a bit, until she appeared to take a deep breath. She apologised but reminded me that we'd had two kisses and that was it.

I'd had it. I walked up to her, grabbed her hands and said, "You're mine." Then I kissed her deeply. I started caressing her cheek while my other hand travelled up her arm. When I got level with her breasts, I pinched one of her nipples and started to play. *God, she feels so good, and she's so responsive.* I then grabbed her butt and pulled her against my erection. I wanted her to feel how she affected me. She gasped as I tweaked some more. I couldn't wait to be inside her, watching as she came around me. Unfortunately, I didn't get my wish as she pushed me away again. *What is it with this woman?*

"Justin, I can't just jump into bed with you. That's not who I am."

As much as I wanted her, I had to respect her for that. I leaned my forehead against hers as I tried to calm myself down. I took her into my arms and just held her for a few minutes. I already had so much respect for Jazmin. She was amazing.

"It's fine, don't worry. Can I take you out for dinner tomorrow night?" I asked.

"OK, but not too late. I'm sure my boss won't be happy if I'm late for work Monday morning. I'm sure he hates me."

"Don't worry about him," I said. *I think he's the one taking funds from the company, so he may be going soon,* I thought to myself. I walked to the door, holding her hand. "I'll pick you up at 5pm tomorrow evening. How's that sound?"

"That's great," she replied.

I left, feeling a lot happier than I had when I arrived. Now, where to take her? I called Marcus and asked him to book somewhere nice to eat for tomorrow. I then hung up and headed back to my car.

I spent the rest of my weekend working on my bike, and thinking of Jazmin. I may run a multibillion-pound corporation, but I had always enjoyed tinkering with engines, and I loved my bikes.

CHAPTER 7

Jazmin: A New Week

Monday morning had come around far too quickly. I was already heading into the office, going through in my head what needed to be done. I was presenting the advert and photos to my client on Friday, so I needed to ensure everything was ready. However, my mind kept going back to last night and the lovely evening I had had with Justin. We had gone to a restaurant I had never been to, and the food was spectacular.

I got in, put my bag away, grabbed a tea, and headed to the editing suite. Jim was already in there, loading up the film for us to go through. It was lunchtime before I came out, and I already had a message from Justin. I pinged him a quick response and grabbed something to eat. And that is how the next few days went: coming into the office, working on the advert, grabbing something to eat, and carrying on.

Wednesday lunchtime came, and I have another message from Justin. We had been texting back and forth a lot and I couldn't wait to see him that evening.

I opened the text and my heart sank. He couldn't make that evening – something about having to fly to France to sort out a problem. He promised that he would make it up to me when he saw me on Friday. I just hope he didn't mean at work, but in the evening. I tried to call him but couldn't get through. I guessed that he was in the air.

I went back to the editing suite to finish off the advert and then checked how Margaret was doing with the photos and presentation. She was doing well so I didn't need to worry about that. I didn't leave till late, and felt really down by the time I got in. It was funny how quickly Justin had worked his way into my soul. I didn't like it; I felt vulnerable, and that was a feeling I fought to stay away from.

The rest of the week went slowly. I texted Justin a couple of times, but didn't hear anything back. I supposed I would see him at the presentation, as he was due to be there. If he turned up, that was.

Friday came around and I still felt down. I'd received nothing from Justin, but I shouldn't have been surprised. That was what usually happened when I liked someone. They flirted with me and said we'd go out, and then ghosted me. It was one of the reasons I kept my secret to myself...

My clients turned up, and I show them into the boardroom. I was just getting ready to start the presentation, when Justin walked in and introduced himself. I decided to ignore him, as he was just not worth it.

The presentation goes well and they approve everything. I leave my clients with Mr Underwood and Justin, as I organise for everything to be published. I could feel Justin's eyes on me (the boardroom is opposite my desk). Once I was done, it was gone 4.30pm and I decided to go home. There was no way I was going to hang around just to have Justin ignore me even more. I said goodbye, wished everyone a good weekend, and walked out the door. I kept trying to remind myself that we were not a couple, so I shouldn't be upset, but it didn't work.

As I was walking towards the train station, a car pulled up beside me. I turned my head as the window slid down, and there he is: the infamous Mr Blake.

"Mr Blake, I'm sorry but I've finished for the week. Any questions will have to wait until Monday." Justin got out of the car and walked over to me.

"I'm sorry. Really, really sorry."

"What have you got to be sorry about? I'm just a woman you spent a little time with – you have no obligations towards me – so no reason to apologise. Now, if you will excuse me, I have a train to catch." I turned to walk away, but Justin took hold of my arm.

"Jazmin, please, give me a chance to explain. We can go to my place, have some dinner, and I'll explain."

"Justin, look, it's OK. You don't need to worry. You've spent a bit of time with a fat bird, so you can give yourself a gold star for that. You can go back to your models now."

"Jazmin, please don't ever put yourself down like that again. It's not like that at all. I want you. Please come for dinner, and let me explain. Please." I stood there for a few minutes, trying to decide if he was being genuine or not. With that very 'cheeky boy' look on his face, I had to say yes.

I got into the back of his car with him, and Fred pulled into the traffic. I sat there feeling nervous, not wanting to say anything. I looked out of the window, and we soon pulled up outside a tall office building, with *Black Corp* on the front.

"I thought we were going to your place?"

"We are. I live in the penthouse here. It gives me a nice, quick journey to work each day." I giggled at Justin's comment and got out of the car. He took my hand and led me to the building. Before long, we were in the lift on our way up. It didn't take long for us to get to the top, but I was glad when we did, as the electricity between us was increasing and I didn't want to do anything stupid.

"Would you like a drink?"

"Water, thank you."

"Wine it is, then."

"Justin, no, I asked for water." I wanted to keep my head straight while in his company. I couldn't trust myself otherwise.

He walked over to the very large kitchen, which was to the right of the living room, and went to the fridge. I followed him and sat on one of the seats in front of the island.

"So, what do you want to say to me?" Justin placed a glass of white wine in front of me and sat on the stool next to me. He took my hands, which I quickly grabbed back.

"Jazmin, I'm truly sorry that I haven't responded to you this week. There was a problem in my Paris office, and then I was trying to confirm who has been stealing from HM."

"Steeling from the company? Oh, my god."

"I couldn't contact you because the person who has been stealing has been trying to make it look like *you* had taken the money."

"What? I would never do that. I swear I have never stolen anything in my life. I can show you proof of all the invoices I have raised and the payments that have been received." Justin put up his hand.

"Jazmin, it's OK, I know you aren't the thief. I can't tell you who is, but you will find out soon enough. I couldn't be seen to be in contact with anyone from your area, so that's why I couldn't reply, or see you on Wednesday."

I sat there in shock, not knowing what to say. I had been considered a thief, and I was lucky that that wasn't still the case. I took a sip of my wine and it tasted divine – crisp and dry, just how I like it. "So, what happens next?" I asked.

"Well, I'm going to ask Chrystal to sort out some dinner for us, and we are going to have a nice quiet evening in."

"I didn't mean about us. I meant about the problem at work."

"I know what you meant, and things will be sorted soon, so there is nothing to worry about."

A middle-aged lady walked in.

"Chrystal, this is Jazmin, my girlfriend." I can only imagine that I had a look of shock on my face because Justin looked at me and grinned.

"Nice to meet you, Miss Jazmin"

"Likewise. And please, call me Jaz – most people do."

"What would you like for dinner?" she asked.

"I would normally have fish and chips as it's Friday, but I don't mind."

"Fish and chips it is, then."

"Why don't we go and sit in comfort, while Chrystal prepares dinner?"

We walked out of the kitchen and into the living room. There were three large and very comfortable-looking black sofas around a fireplace. Justin sat down on one of them and, as I went to sit near him, he pulled me onto his lap.

"So, I'm your girlfriend now, am I?"

"Well, what else would you be?"

"I don't know – your bit on the side? Someone to waste some time with? You tell me."

"I'm so sorry, Jazmin. Please don't be like this. You mean so much to me."

"Just don't ignore me again. Otherwise you won't have me as your girlfriend any more." Justin held his hands up and swore it would never happen again.

"Now, give your man a kiss."

We sat there, kissing and chatting, until Chrystal cleared her throat to let us know she was there.

"Dinner is served."

"Thank you," replied Justin.

I went to get off Justin's lap but he picked me up instead.

"Put me down, I'm too heavy."

"No, you're not." He carried me back to the kitchen, and put me back down on the same stool as before.

The food was delicious and I ate it all. We talked about how Justin got into advertising, and why I chose that direction too. Without even realising, I was already on my second glass of wine, and getting tired.

"I should head home, it's been a long week, and I'm tired."

"Please stay." Justin looked at me with those piercing blue eyes and it made it very difficult to refuse him.

"I don't know."

"No pressure. You can sleep in one of the guest bedrooms, if it makes you more comfortable. It's not a problem. I just want you around. I've missed you." With that said, I made up my mind.

I walked over to him and put my arms around his neck. I rose up onto my tiptoes and said, "That won't be necessary," and kissed him long and hard. He wrapped his arms around me and pulled me closer. I could feel how aroused I made him, and I was very pleased.

We parted, and he took me by the hand and led me through the living room, through a doorway, and down a short hallway. When we got to the end, there were a set of double doors. Justin turned to me and said:

"Are you sure? You can change your mind at any time."

"I'm sure," I replied.

He opened the door and led me into a large, spacious bedroom. It was all decorated in white and grey, and looked very smart. It was warm and comforting, and made me feel relaxed.

Justin pulled me to him and kissed me, our tongues fighting for control. With my hands on his chest, he moved his around to my back. He found the zip to my dress and slowly pulled it down. He then brushed the sleeves over my shoulders and the dress dropped to the floor. I was so glad I wore matching underwear today. I tried to hide myself as I felt embarrassed, but he moved my hands away.

"Don't hide yourself. You're beautiful."

"I don't feel it," I said.

"Well, you are. And don't you forget it."

He then started to suck and nibble on my neck and down to my shoulder while playing with my aching nipples. I moaned softly and started to undo his shirt. He had a smattering of hair over his chest, and very firm abs. He shivered as I lightly scraped my nails down his front. I then slid my hands underneath and over his shoulders, so I could remove his shirt. It gathered around his waist as it was still tucked in. Everything was very slow and tender, and I could already feel the need for him to be inside me. *I am so ready for him.*

Justin slowly stroked a hand down my belly until he reached my knickers. He then slid his hand underneath and went to my nib. "So wet for me already," he says, then gently slid his fingers up and down my slit. I start to shake; I just want him in me.

"Justin, please." I don't know what I'm asking for, but I want it now.

"Be patient, little one," he said.

He slowly walked me backwards while still teasing me, and pushed me up to the bed. Before I knew it, I was flat on my back, edging myself up to the pillows while giggling. I felt like a schoolgirl, and her first time.

Justin crawled up between my legs towards me, kissing his way up the inside of my leg. The anticipation was growing, and I couldn't wait. He got to my knickers.

"I think we can lose these now," he said.

He slowly slid them down and threw them over his shoulder. With a smile on his face, he started to suck and nip at my nib. The pressure was building as he slid two large fingers into me. My fingers tangled into his rich, dark brown hair as my moans increased.

"You're so tight, I can't wait to be in you."

"Then why aren't you?" I said.

"All good things come to those who wait."

I smiled, and continued to rock my hips in time with his fingers. I was so close when he stopped.

"What? Why'd you stop?" I asked.

"Patience, my sweet."

He then stood and removed his shirt and trousers. I could see the top of his manhood poking out of his boxer briefs. He was so big. He caught me staring.

"You will stretch."

"I know, but I've never seen such a big one." I think I had expanded his ego as he had a massive grin on his face. He crawled back over me, and I could feel his member rubbing against me.

"Let's get rid of this bra, shall we?" He quickly unhooked it, took it off, and threw it to join my knickers on the floor. He was now holding himself up on his hands, looking down at me.

"You're beautiful, and don't you ever forget it."

"I'm on the pill. And I'm clear from STI's," I said, and he smiled.

"Good, I hate condoms. I'm clean too, and I want to feel all of you."

Knowing this, he nudged at my entrance and I let him in. It felt amazing; he filled me completely. We laid there, joined together, for a few seconds. He then pushed further into me until he was in up to the hilt.

"Oh, my god, that feels good." I laugh, and we start to move.

I wrapped my legs around his back and pulled him in closer. As the sensations increased, he nibbled on my neck. I scratched my nails down his back, and he groaned. He sped up and you could hear our sweaty bodies slapping together.

"Fuck, oh god, don't stop," I said.

"I have no intention of stopping until you come."

The pressure builds more and more, to the point where I didn't think I could take much more.

"Please, oh please."

"Come for me, my angel."

With just those five words, I exploded around him. I had never had such an intense orgasm in my life. A few more moves and Justin was shouting out my name as he pulsed in me, spilling his seed. He collapsed on top of me, still inside of me, and rolled me over so I was on top of him.

"More? Surely you can't go again that quickly?"

"No, I can't, but give me five and I will. I just want to hold you."

We slowly came down from our euphoria as I played with the hairs on his chest.

"That was amazing. It's never been like that with any other woman." This made me smile. I went to get up, but Justin held me down.

"I need to pee."

"OK, through that door. But don't take too long," he said as he looked down at his already growing member. I smirked and headed to the bathroom.

Again, the room was massive. I was sure I could fit my whole flat in that room. I made myself comfortable, cleaned myself up, and headed back into the bedroom. We spent the next few hours enjoying each other's bodies. I was sure I had never come so much in just one night. The positions, well, just use your imagination. I think it was about 1pm when we finally dropped off to sleep.

I woke up to the sun shining through the windows. (Yes, there are floor-to-ceiling windows in there, too.) I looked to my left, but the bed was empty. I looked around and saw one of Justin's shirts. There was no way I was fitting into that. I got up and headed back into the bathroom. I used his toothbrush, grabbed the bathrobe, and walked out. I saw all my clothes neatly folded on a chair. They looked as though they had been washed. I found my nickers and put them on, and headed out of the room.

As I walked into the living room, I could hear Justin talking, so I followed his voice. He was standing by the window, looking out over London.

"Monday, not today," I heard him say. "I don't want anyone thinking that Jazmin has anything to do with it." He hadn't noticed that I was there, so I continued to stand and listen to the one-sided conversation. He didn't sound happy. "I don't care what the police say. They can go to the office on Monday and arrest him then, not before." This is when he turns around and sees me standing there. "I have to go. Keep me informed." He hung up.

"Is that about the fraud in the office?" I asked.

"It's nothing you need to worry about."

"Justin, tell me, or I'm out that door and you will only see me at work."

"Well, you're a tough cookie, aren't you?"

"Yes. So spill."

"OK, yes, it is about what's happened at HM. You will find out more at work on Monday. I don't want to tell you too much and make it awkward for you, so please just wait and see what happens. OK?"

"OK. But you tell me everything after that?"

"We'll see."

"Fine. Now, what's for breakfast? I'm starving."

We walked into the kitchen, and Justin told me my options. I ended up choosing bacon sandwiches with a cup of tea, and Justin had the same. We ended up spending the whole weekend together (with the exception of ten minutes when he takes me home to change and get some fresh clothes). A lot of it was spent in bed, and I can promise you, I had no complaints.

Sunday evening came, and Justin took me home. He walked me to the door and waited while I let myself in.

"Do you want to come in?" I asked.

"If I come in, I won't leave." I liked the idea, but I did need to get some sleep.

"OK, then. When will I see you next?"

"In the office tomorrow. But how about we try Wednesday again?"

"OK," I replied.

We kissed goodnight, and Justin headed home. I put my stuff away and called Emma. There was no way I was not telling her about my weekend (I just kept out the bit about the police and someone stealing from the company). Once I was off the phone, I took a shower and got ready for bed. I was exhausted and needed some sleep. I got into bed and messaged Justin to say goodnight. He messaged straight back. I was already missing him.

Chapter 8

Jazmin's Shocking Day

Why was it that Monday mornings came around so quickly?

I went to get up, and found I was aching in various different places. Not a bad ache – quite a nice ache, actually. I messaged Justin to tell him what he had done to me, and he came back with a smiley face and, "There's more where that came from." I laughed, and sent him a kissing emoji. I went to get washed and dressed.

I was in the office by 7.30am. The rest of my team were in by 8.30am, and we sat down to go through what work there was, and who would be dealing with which clients' requirements. It was around 9.30am when there appeared to be a disturbance just outside. That was when Justin walked in with several police officers and the manager of HR.

They headed our way but stopped in front of Emma. Justin asked if Mr Underwood was in his office.

"Yes, he is." She stood up, and walked them to his door and let them in. We heard raised voices, and then

Mr Underwood came out shouting, "It's her fault," and pointed my way. We all just sat there, staring, as the police grabbed hold of him and put him in handcuffs.

"Keith Underwood, I hereby arrest you on the charge of fraud and theft of company funds. You do not have to say anything, but it may harm your defence, if you do not mention when questioned, something which you later rely on in court. Anything you do say may be given in evidence." As the police officer read him his rights, Mr Underwood stared at me with a nasty look on his face.

"I'll get you for this," he said to me. I had no idea what he meant. Two of the officers took Keith away, and that left Justin standing with a more senior-looking officer and the HR manager with him, looking around the room.

"Can I have everyone's attention, please? As you have seen, Mr Underwood has been removed from this office. Can I please ask that this is not discussed with *anyone* outside of this room? That does include anyone else in the company who is not in this room, plus your families, friends, and partners. Inspector Taylor and her team will be interviewing each and every one of you in turn. I ask you to please be open and honest with your answers. They will be setting up in the boardroom, so please help them with anything they may need."

Justin showed the officers into the boardroom while we all sat there, stunned.

"What's that all about?" Margaret asked.

"I have no idea. And God only knows what I'm meant to have done to Keith, and what I have to do with all this."

Emma then walked up to us, and the look on her face was one of complete and utter shock.

"I take it you knew absolutely nothing about this?"

"Of course not, I knew nothing about it. He tended to deal with all the money side himself. He would then hand everything over to accounts once he was happy. I tended to only type up his letters and reports. God, I hope I still have a job."

"I wonder for how long this has been going on, and what he's done!" I said, just as Justin came out of the boardroom.

"Miss Cooper, can I have a word, please?"

"Yes, of course, Mr Blake. How can I help?"

"Follow me, please." I followed Justin into Mr Underwood's office. "Close the door, please." I closed the door and turned around. Justin walked straight up to me, and took me in his arms and held me tight.

"Hey, is everything OK?" I asked.

"It's fine. I just needed to hold you. The police would like to talk to you first as Keith seems to have a problem with you."

"Do I need a Solicitor?"

"No, HR will be in there with you."

"Do they know about us?"

"Not yet, but I will talk to them about that when it's my turn."

"OK, I better go in, then."

Justin and I walked out of Mr Underwood's office and headed to the boardroom.

"This is Miss Cooper. Miss Cooper, this is Inspector Taylor. Please assist as much as possible. Heather is here as your representative, should you need one."

"Thank you, Mr Blake. How can I help you, Inspector?" I said as I sat down next to Heather from HR. Justin left the room and closed the door behind him.

"So, Miss Cooper, how long have you known Mr Underwood?"

"Please, call me Jaz. He came into the department about two years ago. He worked in accounts before that, but I didn't know him then, so about two years."

"And what was your relationship with Mr Underwood?"

"He's my boss. I report directly to him – or should I say, I did."

"What about after work? Did you spend any time together outside of the office?"

"No, not at all. It is, or was, purely a professional relationship."

"Have you ever had any problems with Mr Underwood? Any disagreements, misunderstandings – anything like that?" I sat there for a few minutes, thinking.

"The only thing I can think of was soon after he moved into this role. I used to have his office and his was next to mine. One day, I was working late and he came in to see me. He walked around to my side of the desk and started flirting with me. I wasn't interested, and I was seeing someone at the time. He started getting closer and put his hand on my knee. Again, I explained I wasn't interested, and was there anything else I could help him with. He called me a cock blocker and a bitch, and walked out. The next day, when I got in, he had had all my things moved out of my office and put on a spare desk. He had also had all his things moved into that same office. After that day, he always seemed to have a problem with me. I just tried to keep out of his way."

"Well, thank you for your time, Jaz. That will be all for now."

I walked out of the room feeling exhausted. As the day went on, more members of my team, and others around us, were taken into the room to be questioned. By the end of the day, they had spoken to about half of us. I was glad to get out of the building and back to my flat. I texted Justin to see how he was, and then we spoke for about an hour. We didn't talk about work, as I had to remind him that he had said we were not to talk to anyone about this outside of the office. He had chuckled and changed the subject.

For the next few days, more people were interviewed and some questioned again. Justin came in on Wednesday, and was in with the inspector for over an hour. When he left, he looked my way, smiled and lifted his phone. A few minutes later, my phone pinged. It was Justin just checking that I was still on for dinner that night. I couldn't wait; I wanted to know what was happening. I told him I was, and he confirmed that he'd meet me outside at 5.30pm.

The rest of the day dragged. The Inspector asked me a few more questions about the incident with Mr Underwood, and told me that they would be charging him with harassment as well. I didn't really know how I felt about that, but when they said that I wasn't the only one, I didn't feel so bad.

5.30pm finally came, so I packed up, said goodbye to the few people that were still in, and walked out of the office. Fred was standing by the side of the SUV, ready to open the door, when I walked out of the building. I got in, and there was Justin, looking as handsome as ever.

"So, Justin, what's going on?"

"Hello to you too, my sweet."

"I'm sorry. Hello. So, what's going on?"

"As you reminded me the other day, we cannot talk about it just now."

"OK." I gave Justin a kiss on the cheek.

"Call that a kiss?" He pulled me towards him and gave me a proper kiss. I lost all train of thought; it was all sensation. When we finally parted, I was breathless.

"How was your day?" Justin asked.

"Oh, it was OK. Isn't there anything you can tell me about what's happening?"

"All I can say is that there is plenty of evidence against him. One thing though, he really has it in for you. If he gets bail, you're moving in with me so I can keep you safe."

"That won't be necessary. I'm completely capable of looking after myself. Now, where are we eating tonight? I've hardly eaten today and I'm starving."

"Jazmin, don't you go changing the subject. I mean what I say: I want you safe."

"I know you do, but it's not necessary and stop calling me Jazmin."

"It's your name, isn't it?"

"Yes, but you know I prefer Jaz."

We went to a lovely little Italian restaurant, and sat and chatted while eating. He told me about his parents, and that he had a brother.

"I'll introduce you to them on Sunday. We've been invited to lunch at my parents' place."

"What? No, it's too soon. We've only been seeing each other for a couple of weeks."

"Then I had better take you out every night until then." He smiled and kissed my hand.

We finished our meal and went for a walk along the river. It was a lovely evening, and we were not the only people enjoying the area.

"I would love to have a house by the river. I know there's always the risk of flooding, but it's just so tranquil."

"Then one day we will."

"I could never afford the repayments." I tried to ignore the 'we' comment. *He'll soon get bored of me*, I thought.

We walked back to the car and got in the back.

"So, what about your family?" Justin asked.

"There's not much to tell. They were killed on my 18th birthday. I stayed with Emma and her family until everything was sorted out, and then I bought my studio flat. I've been there ever since."

"I'm so sorry."

"Don't be – they weren't very nice parents. They were never there for me, and missed every birthday. I don't even know why they had me."

"No brothers or sisters?"

"No, I'm an only child, which is probably a good thing. Otherwise, there would have been two of us being ignored. I'm just glad I met Emma. Her family have become my family."

We pulled up outside my place and he walked me to my door.

"I'm sorry you had such a hard time, but you have me now, and I'm not going anywhere."

I smiled and gave him a hug and kiss goodnight. As I closed the door, I wished I could believe what Justin had just said. I could imagine my life with him already, even after only a short time.

CHAPTER 9

Justin's Plans

I left Jazmin looking a little sad. I didn't like that at all. I was starting to get a funny sensation in my chest whenever I thought of her. It was a nice feeling, but I didn't know what it meant. What I did know was that I would do everything in my power to make her happy.

Everything she had told me about her parents' death and what happened after, I already knew. She hadn't said anything though about how ill she had been, and I didn't know about how her parents had treated her. She'd been through so much, I was not going to let the Underwood issue hurt her.

Fred drove me home, and I started on my emails. I got a text from Jazmin to say goodnight, so I replied back saying the same. She always brought a smile to my face, and seemed to take all my worries away without even trying. I called Mum and Dad to confirm Sunday, and went to bed. As I laid there, I wondered if Jazmin would move in with me, regardless of the Underwood issue. I enjoyed having her here, and missed her when she wasn't. I made a mental note to ask her on Friday night. I then closed my eyes and drifted off to sleep.

Thursday came, and I spent a great deal of it in meetings downstairs. I wanted to get over to Hammonds, but it wasn't until 5pm that I was finally on my way. I arrived at 5.30pm as Inspector Taylor and her team were walking out the door.

"How's it all going?" I asked.

"It's going well. I don't think we will need to come back now – we have enough to go forward. You have a good team here. Look after them." They then left, and I walked in and up to the first floor.

There weren't many people left, just a few packing up. I couldn't see Jazmin anywhere, so I checked with Emma, who was still at her desk.

"She left a little while ago."

I knew Emma had been told about Jazmin and I, so I wasn't concerned when I saw the knowing look on her face.

"Mr Blake, what's going to happen to me? With Mr Underwood gone, I have no person to support."

"Don't worry about that. There will be a new manager soon."

"OK. Thank you."

"No problem."

I walked back out the door and rang Jazmin's number.

"Hi," she said.

"Where are you?"

"I'm on the train, on my way home. Why?"

"I've just got to your office to pick you up."

"You didn't say anything, otherwise I would have waited," she replied.

"I did tell you that we would go out every day up to Sunday."

"Sorry, I didn't think you meant it. You are more than welcome to come over, and I'll cook us dinner."

"That sounds like a great idea. I'm on my way."

I jumped back in the car and Fred drove me to Jazmin's place. She was just arriving when we pulled up.

"Is my overnight bag in the boot?" I asked Fred.

"Yes, Sir," he replied.

"Great, I'll have it please. And can you bring the Lexus LFA down for the morning, please?"

"Of course, Sir. Shall I drop the keys into the post box, or should I bring them up?" Fred asked.

"Bring them up, please."

"I'll be back as soon as possible, Sir."

"Thank you," I said. I walked up to Jazmin with my bag.

"Hoping to stay, are we?" she asked.

"Well, it seems such a shame not to be able to join you in this bottle of wine." I held up one of my favourite wines, and grin.

"I'm sure Fred would be more than happy to pick you up," she replied.

"It's his night off."

"Really?"

We walked through the door and headed up the stairs. Jazmin made a simple chicken stir-fry for dinner. It was delicious, and the wine went with it well.

"I'll wash up as you cooked," I say.

"We can both do it," she replies.

I washed while Jazmin dried and put away. It didn't take long. We then curled up to a film. It was the best film ever (as neither of us got to see much of it!).

Chapter 10

Jazmin's Time to Play

Justin had come over for dinner and we were just sitting down to watch a film. I chose *The Holiday*. I knew it was not Christmas, but it was one of my favourite films. He started to nibble at my neck.

"I thought we were watching the film?"

"We are, but I'm examining your neck as well. You do have a beautiful neck."

He pulled me onto his lap and continued kissing and nibbling. I decided that this time I was going to be in control. I got up from his lap and moved the coffee table out of the way. Justin raised his eyebrow, questioning, but I just carried on. I got on my hands and knees and crawled between his legs.

Once there, I slowly walked my fingers up his legs. I got to his knees and then started to massage the inside of his thighs. I could see that the area I was aiming for was already growing. I knelt up and when I got to his crutch, I started to rub. Justin went to put a hand on my breast, but I slapped it away.

"Oh no you don't."

I continued to gently rub him as I started to undo his fly. His member was hard and pulsing as I started to caress him. I wrapped my hand firmly around the base and started to move up and down. He groaned, and started to move his hips. I lowered my head and took him into my mouth, and swirled my tongue around his tip. I then sucked him hard as I pumped him more and more. He grabbed my head and pushed himself to the back of my throat. I carried this on, until:

"Oh shit, Jaz. Oh my god. Fuck." That was when I stopped, stood up, and walked away. "What the hell, Jazmin?"

I turned around, walking backwards to the bed.

"Oh, you little minx."

"Then you had better do something about it." I continued walking backwards towards my bed, but now Justin was following me. Once I got there, I worked my way up and laid down. Justin climbed up over me.

"So, my little minx, it's my turn."

"Oh, goody," I said.

Justin started by unbuttoning my blouse, and removed it, then my skirt. I had stockings on, of which I think he approved. He worked his way down my body, kissing and nipping as he went. He got to my nickers and pulled them down.

"We won't be needing these." He then started to blow gently on my nib while playing with one of my nipples. He then spread my lips, and started to suck and lick me out. "Always so ready for me, my little minx." I groaned, and ran my fingers through his hair. It was my turn to start to move my hips.

Justin hitched one of my legs over his shoulder and then started to insert two fingers into me.

"Is this what you want, my little minx?" he asked.

"Is that my name now?" I said with a moan.

"Why? Don't you like it? I bet you like this," he said as he pushed a third finger into me and sucked on my nib. I was so close.

"Oh god, fuck, oh fuck. Don't stop." That was when Justin stopped, just like I had. "Shit."

"Something wrong, my love?"

"No. Everything is just fine."

He then slowly worked his way up my body, leaving trails of kisses as he went. I was so desperate for him to be inside me but I tried not to show it. We were now face to face, and he was nudging at my entrance. I wrapped my legs around him and pushed. He went deep into me and I almost burst; the sensation was out of this world. We both stayed still for a few seconds, and then we started to move. Our bodies glistened with sweat as we moved as one, matching each other stroke for stroke. "Harder," I said, so he swivelled his hips and pushed harder and further than I thought possible. "Oh, Justin."

"Come for me, Jazmin," and just with those four words I was over the edge and falling hard. One more push and Justin called out my name as he reached his release. He collapsed on top of me as I laid there in a euphoric state. Justin rolled off me and pulled me to him. "Oh, my god, Jazmin."

"Hmm," is all I could say as I drifted off to sleep in Justin's arms.

The next few days went by in a blur. Friday was busy in the office, and on Saturday Justin flew me to Paris. We went on his private jet which was amazing. I had never been in such luxury. I was trying not to get too used to it as I was sure he would dump me once he was bored with me.

We had a private tour up the Eiffel Tower and dinner at some upper-class restaurant. It was all just so breath taking. When we got back, Justin took me to his place.

"You might as well stay with me as we are off to my parents' tomorrow."

"That's fine. But I don't have a change of clothes."

"That's not a problem. I'll get some delivered."

"What do you mean, delivered?" I asked.

"I have a personal shopper. I'll ask her to bring a few outfits over and some nightwear."

"It's 11pm at night – nothing's open."

"It is for me," he replied. Justin took his phone out of his pocket and tapped something into the screen. After a short pause, someone answered at the other end. "Charlie, it's Justin. I need some nightwear, underwear, and some outfits for meeting my parents. How quickly can you get them to me? Hmm, OK. 18. Yes, that's great. See you soon.

"Right, Charlie will be here in 30 minutes, so just enough time for a drink."

"Now, I know my dress size isn't in my personnel file, so how do you know it?" I asked. Justin stood there looking at me with a smirk on his face.

"I have undressed you several times in the last few weeks." That made me laugh.

"I suppose you're right there, but you weren't exactly looking at my clothing."

"I wasn't, was I?"

That was when the ding of the lift went, and a very elegant lady stepped off with a rack of clothing.

"Thanks for this, Charlie; especially at such a late hour."

"It's not a problem, Mr Blake. You pay me very well to come when you need me. Where should I put all of this?" she asked.

"Please follow Jazmin to my bedroom. You can go through everything with her there."

I went to shake hands with Charlie. "Lovely to meet you, and thank you for this."

"That's not a problem," she replied.

"Please, follow me." I led Charlie to Justin's bedroom, and took a look at the clothes. They were all designer garments and very beautiful. They still had the price tags on them, so I snuck a look. Then I wish I hadn't, as it was going to take me years to pay him back. I chose the minimum of items, thanked Charlie, and walked back out to the living room where Justin was waiting. "Thank you again, Charlie," I said, as Charlie came out with the remainder of the clothing.

"That's my pleasure."

"Hold on," Justin said. "What about these other garments? Why is Charlie taking them? Don't they fit?"

"Justin, they all fit beautifully, but they are very expensive, so I have selected what I need to get me through until I go home tomorrow."

"The cost isn't an issue, Jazmin, so keep them."

"It is to me. I can't afford to pay you back."

"I didn't ask you to. They're a gift." I could see he was getting a little angry, but I stood my ground.

"Please, Justin. I don't feel right taking them."

"Charlie, please leave the others, and thank you for coming."

"Not a problem, Mr Blake. I'm happy to help." Charlie then left the other items and got back into the lift. I was not happy with the fact that Justin had ignored me and how I felt about taking those 'gifts', as he liked to put it.

"Justin, how could you do that? Just ignore my feelings like that?"

"Don't be silly, Jaz, they're just a gift."

"Justin, I'm not being silly. I'm mad at you for disrespecting me. I'm going to bed. Where's your guest bedroom, please?"

"I'm sorry, Jazmin, I meant no disrespect. I just want to give you everything. I'd give you the world, if I could."

"I don't want the world; I just want you. Can't you see that?" Justin walked up to me and rested his forehead against mine. We looked into each other's eyes. "OK, but please, no more big gifts like this." Justin smirked.

"I can't promise that, what with your birthday coming up."

"How do you know that?"

"It's in your file."

"Oh yeah, I forgot you have access to all my info." My birthday was fifth August, so about five or six weeks away. I had every intention of forgetting about it again this year, but I had a feeling I wouldn't be allowed to. "Anyway, it's very late, and I'm tired. I really don't want big bags under my eyes when I meet your family tomorrow – or should I say, later today."

"You will look as beautiful as always, but yes, time for bed."

CHAPTER 11

Jazmin Meets the Parents

When I woke up the next morning, Justin was wrapped around me. I had to admit, I did like waking up with him; I seemed to sleep more soundly. I slowly turned around to face him, and he opened his eyes.

"Hey, baby, did you sleep well?"

"I did, thank you. And you?"

"Yes, I did. Now I can think of another good reason to wake up together." As Justin moved his hand from my hip to my bum and pulled me closer, he was already hard and raring to go.

"I bet you can," I replied. We made love before we got up and headed to the shower.

We were not due at Justin's parents' house until 1pm, so we had a leisurely breakfast, sitting on the balcony by the living room.

"I hope your parents like me. I'm not exactly your normal sort of date."

"They'll love you. And even if they don't, it doesn't matter, as I have no intention of letting you go."

We headed off to get ready to leave.

We we're in the car by noon, with Fred driving. Justin had explained that his parents lived in Oxshott and his brother and his wife, lived just down the road in Cobham, and that they would be joining us. I sat quietly, looking out the window. I was so nervous.

We pulled up to a set of double gates just after 1pm. As the gates opened, I glimpsed a beautiful mansion with red bricks and marble columns either side of the front door. There was a beautiful garden in front of it with a sweeping driveway. It was stunning.

As Fred pulled the car up in front of the house, the doors opened and a very elegant lady stepped out. She had dark hair, just like Justin's, but she was not as tall. She was slender and very beautiful. We got out, and she rushed over.

"Justin! It's about time you came to see us."

"Mum, give me a break, you know how busy I've been." Justin wrapped her in his arms and kissed her head. "Mum, I'd like you to meet Jazmin, my girlfriend."

"It's a pleasure to meet you, Mrs Blake."

"Oh, please, call me Libbie. I've been looking forward to meeting you. Justin has told me a lot about you."

"All good, I hope."

"Of course. Come in, both of you."

We followed Libbie into the house. As we walked into the large lobby, Libbie shouted out:

"Michael, they're here." A very tall and distinguished-looking man with speckled grey hair came out of a room to our left. There was a sweeping staircase in front of us with what looked like marble stairs. Above us was the most breath taking chandelier, I had ever seen. Each individual crystal glinted in the sunlight, leaving rainbows playing around the walls. There was also a gallery visible upstairs which I presumed led to the bedrooms.

We are led through some double doors to our right which brought us into a spacious living room. Justin's brother and sister-in-law were already there.

"Jazmin," said Libbie, "this is my other son, Andrew, and his wife, Melanie. Andrew, Mel, this is Jazmin, Justin's girlfriend."

"About time too," Andrew said as he walked up to me and took me in a bear hug. "It's so good to finally meet you."

"And you," I said.

"Please, take a seat." Libbie guided me to one of the sofas, and Justin sat next to me. "So, Jazmin, what do your parents do?" Libbie asked.

"They died when I was 18." I replied.

"I'm so sorry, I didn't know. Justin, why didn't you tell me?"

"Libbie, it's OK. We didn't get on, and it is almost six years ago now."

"Well, you have a new family now, so don't you worry."

"What do you do?" asked Andrew as he tried to change the subject.

"I'm a marketing coordinator. I work with a team of six, and we help companies with their advertising and marketing for new products. It's with Hammond Marketing, the company Justin has recently taken over."

"That's how we met," said Justin. "We got talking when she showed me around."

Libbie smiled. "How lovely." Just then, there was a slight cough from behind us.

"Dinner is served." An elderly gentleman stood by the door in what appeared to be a butler's outfit.

"That's wonderful. Shall we all go through?" Michael asked. We all went to stand, and followed Michael and Libbie through to another very spacious and elegantly decorated room. Michael sat at the head of the table, with Libbie at the other end. Justin and I sat to his right, and Andrew and Melanie to his left.

The food was delightful; beautifully made and elegantly displayed. I lost count after the fourth course, but the conversation was light and everyone was so friendly. I did notice though that Andrew ate very little, and Melanie was very attentive towards him – almost overly so. I made a mental note to ask Justin about it when we were next alone.

By the end of the afternoon, I had both Melanie's and Libbie's numbers, and a promise to see them all again soon. As we went to leave, Libbie gave me a big hug.

"Now, don't you go being a stranger, you hear me?"

"I hear you," I said to Libbie, and hugged her back. "I'm sure we'll see you all again soon, and thank you again for such a lovely afternoon."

"It's our pleasure." We got in the car and Fred pulled away.

"Did you have a good time?"

"I did, thank you, Justin. You have a great family. You're very lucky. I hope you don't think me rude, but what's wrong with Andrew?" Justin was quiet for a few minutes before he answered:

"He hasn't been well for a while. I keep asking him about it, but all he says is that it's in hand. I've spoken to Mum and Dad, and they were going to talk to him about it before he leaves."

"I hope everything is OK."

"So, do I," he replied.

We sat in silence for the rest of the journey. I wondered if I should say anything about my abilities – I could help, or at least tell them what was wrong. My powers gave the ability, to sense what was wrong. Almost like a diagnosis of sorts. But I was scared and I hadn't known Justin very long, so felt unsure whether to intrust him with such a secret.

We pulled up outside my place around 6pm, and Justin got out and went around to open my door.

"Let me walk you to your door."

"Not tonight. You need to find out what is happening with your brother. I'll be fine." Justin kissed me goodbye and stood by the car as I walked to the main door. I gave him a wave, and walked through the door and headed to my flat. Just as I pushed open the door, someone pushed me through. I fell and banged my head on the kitchen counter. It knocked me out.

When I came to I was tied up on the floor. My head hurt and I had a metallic taste in my mouth. I slowly turned my head, and that was when I saw him. He was sitting on one of the stools by my kitchen counter. It was Keith Underwood, my former boss. I knew he had been released after questioning, but didn't expect to see him any time soon.

"Keith, why are you here? What am I doing tied up?"

"You ruined my life, so I'm going to ruin yours."

"How have I ruined your life? You were the one who stole from the company, and tried to frame me. I had nothing to do with it."

"You had everything to do with it. I was doing perfectly well where I was. You then rejected the promotion, so I was moved. It made it harder for me to sort things out. You also started to track your team's accounts. You've taken everything from me now."

"Keith, you are only making things worse for yourself. Kidnapping is not going to go down well."

"Who said anything about kidnapping? You're running away with me – or that's how it's going to look."

I was starting to get scared; Keith wasn't making any sense. My head was killing me, but I didn't want to risk using my abilities as I tended to glow when I did. Instead, I just sat on the floor, trying to stay awake. "For how long was I unconscious?" *If it's been a long time, Justin might try to contact me. I usually send him a goodnight message.*

"A couple of hours. Why? Going somewhere?"

"No. I was just wondering." He walked up to me, grabbed my hair, and pulled me up onto my feet.

"No one is coming to save you, not even that fancy boyfriend of yours. You've just dumped him – by text of course – just to make things worse." He had such a crazy smile on his face. What was I going to do? Just then, he slapped me across the face and grabbed my cheeks. "You ready for a little ride, young lady?" he asked.

"I'm not going anywhere with you," I said as I struggled to get free. I could see my phone on the coffee table near me. If only I could get him to let go, I could try to grab my phone and lock myself in the bathroom. He was shaking me now.

"Are you listening to me?"

"Oh, I'm listening," I said as I raised my leg up to knee him hard in the groan. It worked; he fell to the floor and curled up, holding himself. Luckily, my hands were tied at the front, so I grabbed my phone and ran. Just as I was grabbing the handle to the bathroom, Keith grabbed me and pulled me to the ground.

"You bitch. That hurt."

"It was meant to!" I shouted as I tried to kick him. He was now crawling over me. I started to yell for help, hoping that one of my neighbours would hear me. I struggled as well but to no avail. *Shit, this is not going well.*

Keith pinned me down and slapped me again. He tried to kiss me but I moved my head to the side. "Get off of me, you creep."

"What's that boyfriend of yours got that I don't, eh"

"Manners, for a start!" I yelled.

"Well, I think it's time you and I left." He got up off of me and started to pull me back onto my feet. "You won't be needing that," he said as he took my mobile away from me.

All of a sudden, my front door came flying open, and there stood Justin. He came running over and pulled Keith away from me, then punched him squarely in the face. He landed flat on his back, unconscious. "Jazmin, are you OK? You're bleeding. The police are on their way."

"Justin, thank God you're here." Justin untied me and helped me to the sofa. That was when the police and an ambulance arrived. As you can guess, it was some time before I got the chance to talk properly to Justin.

I spoke to the police to give my statement, and then the paramedic wanted me to go to the hospital, due to my head wound. I couldn't exactly tell them that I could fix it myself, so I went. Justin stayed with me the whole time, holding my hand, and telling me that everything would be OK.

"I'll make sure that Keith gets put away for a long time for what he's done to you."

We were sitting in one of the cubicles at the hospital, waiting for all my results to come back.

"Justin, what made you come over?" I asked.

"After I received your text, I didn't know what to think. It didn't seem like something you would do – dump me by text that is. I responded back asking to talk, but you just ignored me."

"You do know that it was Keith who sent the message, not me?"

"I know now. After a while, I started to get this really strong feeling that you needed me, so I came over. As I was walking towards the entrance to your building, I saw Keith at one of your windows. I called the police straightaway and ran up the stairs. You know the rest."

"I'm so glad you came. I had managed to grab my phone, and was trying to get to the bathroom to lock myself in there and phone you when you came through the door. Thank you so much for not believing that message. (*I had been calling him in my mind, but didn't expect it to work*). I don't know what I would have done if you hadn't turned up when you did. He was in the process of trying to take me somewhere, but I don't know where."

"It doesn't matter now. You're safe. You can stay with me until your door is fixed, and I've sorted out some security for the building."

"Thank you, but you don't need to do that."

"It's that, or I move everything of yours to my place. Your choice."

"OK, I accept for now, but I'm helping with the cost."

"We'll see," he replied.

Just then, a nurse walked in.

"Miss Cooper, can I have a word in private, please?" As I had a feeling I knew what it was about, and I didn't want Justin to find out that way, I turned to face him.

"Do you mind?"

"No, not at all. I have a few calls to make, so I'll be back in a short while." Justin gave me a kiss on the cheek, and walked out and away from my cubicle. The nurse walked up beside me.

"It's about some of your results. Your blood work is rather unusual. Do you have any abilities?"

And there it is: the question I had been waiting for.

"Yes, I'm a healer. But my boyfriend doesn't know yet, so please don't say anything in front of him."

"Is that why you didn't heal yourself? You don't want anyone to know?"

"Something like that. I found out when I was 18, and it hasn't been easy for me since then, so I just keep it to myself."

"I can understand that. It's a very rare ability. Well, if you ever need a job, please come and see me. There is always a space for a healer here and, by your results, I'd say that you are very powerful."

"Thank you, I'll keep that in mind."

"You have a slight concussion, but otherwise you're OK. I take it that you would like me to stitch up the wound?"

"If you wouldn't mind? I know it seems silly, but I'm not ready to tell anyone yet."

"That's fine, don't worry. I'll be back in a jiffy to stitch you up, and then you're free to go."

"That's great, thank you."

Just then, Justin poked his head around the curtain.

"Is it safe for me to come back in?"

"Yes, it's fine," I said. "They just need to stitch me up and then we can go."

"Great. I'll call Fred to come and pick us up."

It took another 30 minutes to get us out of the door. By the time we got back to Justin's place, it was 4am in the morning, and I was exhausted.

"Right, missy, off to bed. No work for the next few days. You need to rest."

"I need to work. With no boss, there's lots to do."

"Your team can handle it, so no work."

"Justin, I can't just pick and choose like you can. I need to be in the office. I'll rest today, but I'm going back in tomorrow." I gave him a determined stare and then walked towards his bedroom.

"We'll see," was all he said as he followed me.

When I eventually woke up, the space next to me was empty and the sun was already high in the sky. I got up and went to the bathroom to use the toilet. I looked in the mirror and saw a dark bruise over the top of my right eye. *Oh, how I wish I could just clear it up*. But I knew I couldn't. I walked back into the bedroom, threw on some clothes I had left there, and headed off to look for Justin. He was nowhere to be seen. Chrystal is in the kitchen though so I went to see her.

"Hi, Chrystal."

"Jaz, you're up. How are you feeling?"

"I'm OK, thanks. My head is a little sore, but that's it. Is Justin at work?"

"Oh no, dear, he's in his study, on the phone. I'm sure he'll be out soon. Would you like something to eat? It's lunchtime but I can do you some pancakes, if you would prefer?"

"Lunchtime? I haven't called the office. They will be wondering where I am," I replied.

"I called them earlier," came a rather deep and sexy voice from behind me. "I said you wouldn't be back until later in the week."

"You said what? Justin, we talked about this last night. I'm going back tomorrow."

"Is lunch ready, Chrystal?"

"Yes, Sir, it is."

"Great. We'll have it on the balcony."

"Justin, you're ignoring me again. You know what happens when you do that."

"Sorry, Jazmin. I just want to keep you safe."

"I know, but Keith is in prison, and I'm doing fine."

We walked out onto the balcony, with Chrystal following behind. She had made us a chicken salad with a spicy mayo dressing. It had me drooling. We sat down and started to eat.

"I'm sorry if I'm being a little controlling, but your safety is paramount to me."

"Thank you, but it's not necessary. Why are you so obsessed with my safety?"

"Because you're everything to me. I don't know what I would do if something happened to you."

Over the next few days I stayed at Justin's place. He worked from home to make sure I was OK, and finally let me go back to work on Thursday. The bruising was looking 'beautiful' by then, so I got a few questions.

"Emma," I call from across the office, "how are things going?"

"I should be asking you that question."

"I'm fine – healing well. What's been going on here, then?"

"Nothing special. Drinks after work to catch up, then?"

"That sounds like a good plan to me." I went back to my desk and carried on working.

I stayed at Justin's until the end of the week and then I headed back to my place. I felt a little scared, knowing what had happened, but I was determined to not let that affect me. I would not let Keith scare me out of my own home.

CHAPTER 12

Jazmin's Life Falls Apart

Over the next month, Justin and I saw more and more of each other. We even had a few double dates with Emma and Shawn. It was on one of those double dates – the one for my birthday – when everything went terribly wrong.

We'd been out for a wonderful meal, which Justin insisted on paying for.

"That was absolutely lovely," I said to everyone. "How about we go back to mine? I have a bottle of bubbly in the fridge."

"That sounds like a good idea," said Emma.

"Anything you want, my little minx," said Justin.

"When are you going to stop calling me that?" I asked him.

"Oh, I don't know; some time in the future." He had been speaking about our future a lot lately. It made me feel all gooey inside.

We got a taxi and arrived back at my place about 11pm. After the incident with Keith, the front door was now locked with cameras and better lighting. We even had a proper reception area with a concierge. I thought this was a little OTT, but Justin insisted.

I let us all in and wished Steve, the concierge, a good evening, and headed up to my place. I unlocked my front door and we all headed in.

"So, who wants what?" I asked, as everyone made themselves comfortable. "I have champagne, red and white wine, beer, or tea and coffee. I probably have gin and vodka as well." Everyone asked for bubbly, and Justin came to help me with the glasses.

"Happy birthday, Jazmin."

"Thank you, everyone."

Emma and I were sitting on the floor, leaning against our respective partners chatting, while the men were sat on the sofa talking about football. I was having the best birthday that I had ever had. We were happily chatting away, with bottles and glasses on the coffee table next to us. The next thing I knew, bottles and glasses were flying, and Emma was holding her hand.

"Emma, what have you done?"

She showed me and her hand was bleeding quite badly. Shawn jumped up, looking for something to wrap around it.

"I'll take her to hospital," Shawn said.

"I'll get Fred to take you," said Justin.

"That's not necessary, she doesn't need to go to hospital," I said.

"What? Why?" Justin asked.

"Emma, come here. This is something I should have told you a long time ago, but I was scared."

Emma gave me a funny look and then put her hand in one of mine. I then covered her hand with my other one and closed my eyes. I knew our hands were glowing, and I could feel a familiar warmth as I healed her hand. Once I was done, I let go of her hand and opened my eyes. Everyone was standing there, looking at me.

"What the...? How long have you been able to do that?" Emma asked.

"Since I was 18," I said, quietly.

"Since you were 18? And you didn't think I was good enough to be told?" Emma's voice was rising with each word she said. I thought she would be a little upset, but not this bad. "So, you have known for the last six years and you didn't think you could trust me enough to tell me?"

"It wasn't like that," I started to say, but Emma grabbed her things.

"Shawn, we're leaving."

"Emma, please let me explain." Emma ignored me and walked to the door. "Shawn, please listen. I didn't mean to hurt you guys." She walked out the door with Shawn close behind her. I turned to Justin, hoping for some support, but as soon as I saw the look on his face, I knew I was not going to get any. "Justin, I've only known you a few months, so surely you can understand why I haven't said anything to you?"

"So, you could have healed yourself after the attack?"

"Yes."

"Do you have any other powers?"

"Honestly? I don't know. I don't tend to use my healing abilities very often, so I haven't tried to see if I can do anything else."

Justin just stood in the middle of the living room, staring at me. I felt lost and alone. I just wanted him to take me in his arms and tell me that everything would be OK, but he didn't.

"It's late. I'm going to head home."

"I thought you were staying tonight?" I asked.

"I have work to do. I'll see you in the office." He picked up his things and headed for the door. I was losing everything by just simply using my powers.

"Justin, please don't leave like this. Can't I see you tomorrow? We can talk some more before work on Monday."

"I'm busy. As I said, I'll see you in the office." He walked out the door, slamming the door behind him; no kiss; not even a second glance.

I spent the rest of the weekend curled up on my bed in tears. I didn't know how many texts I sent to Emma and Justin, but neither of them had responded to me. I re-ran the conversations I had with them both, over and over in my head, trying to see if I could have dealt with things differently, but I couldn't come up with anything.

Monday morning came, and I made my way into the office. I sat quietly at my desk, hoping that I would get to see them both soon. Lunchtime came and went, but there was no sign of either of them. That was how it went for the next few days – me sitting at my desk wishing one of them would show their face, but neither of them did.

Wednesday afternoon came, and I was starting to get really worried. I was about to text Emma again when my office phone rang.

"Good afternoon, Jazmin Cooper speaking."

"Jazmin, its Rachel from HR. Can you please come and see me?"

"Now?"

"Yes, please."

"OK. I'll be right up." I hung up and headed to the stairs. It only took me a minute to reach Rachel, who was waiting for me outside one of the meeting rooms.

"Jazmin, thank you for coming. Please come in and take a seat." Rachel followed and closed the door. I sat down, wondering what it was all about.

"As you are aware, a few months ago we were taken over by The Blake Corporation. The new owner has now decided to merge Hammond Marketing with his main business. Unfortunately, this means some redundancies are inevitable."

"OK. Who out of my team is going?" I asked.

"I'm afraid it's not anyone in your team that's going." Rachel sat there staring at me as the message sank in. I was being made redundant. No wonder he was not replying to my messages; he was getting rid of me, the bastard.

"Oh, I see. How long do I have?"

"If you could clear your desk by the end of the day and leave your pass with security that would be great."

"What? I'm not even being given time to find a new job? What am I meant to do? Aren't you meant to give me time for interviews, and a redundancy offer?"

"All the information, including your severance pay, is in this letter." Rachel handed me a sealed envelope.

"Is anyone else being made redundant?" I asked.

"I'm not at liberty to say."

"What about Emma Slowne? I haven't seen her all week."

"She's been moved to the head office of The Blake Corporation already, as will those who are staying. As there are others who will be going, could I please ask for you to not say anything just yet? I appreciate this is all very sudden and you have no reason to keep quiet, but I would appreciate your co-operation in this."

I couldn't believe what I was hearing, she's right that it's all very sudden and I have every reason to speak out, but I just agreed, so I could get out of there, as quickly as possible.

I walked out of the meeting, pissed as hell. So, he was firing me but putting it down as redundancy so I didn't sue. I walked back down the stairs and went to my desk. I started to clear everything out of the draws and threw away what I didn't need. Luckily, I kept a bag in one of the draws for when I went shopping at lunchtime. I put my stuff in the bag, and cleared down my laptop and left it on the desk.

"What are you doing?" Margaret asked.

"Leaving." I replied. Margaret came up to me.

"Jaz, what's happened?"

"Let's just say I won't be going out with Mr Blake anymore."

"I'm so sorry. I thought things were going well?"

"So, did I, but apparently not." Margaret gave me a big hug.

"Keep in touch, and I'll let you know what's going on around here."

"Thanks, Margaret, but I don't think I want to know. I think he just wants me gone, so I doubt anything else will happen."

"You should sue."

"How? And with what? It doesn't matter, it was time for me to move on, anyway." I finished packing and walked to the stairs. I turned and took one last look around, and off I went. I couldn't believe he had done this to me. I headed down the stairs, leaving my pass with security, and started to head home. It wasn't until I found myself standing in front of my door that

I started to cry. How could everything have gone so wrong in such a short amount of time? I got in and dumped my stuff on the floor. I grabbed my phone and dropped onto the sofa. *If he thinks I'm going quietly, he's got another thing coming.*

I opened the envelope and read what was inside. It was your standard letter, but I had to look twice at the amount of redundancy pay I was getting. I'd only been with the company for five and a half years, so I didn't expect much, but the figure had far too many zeros – five, to be precise. He was paying me £200,000 to go. *That can't be right. I can't take it.* I unlocked my phone and started to type out a message to Justin:

So, I take it we're over? And you're paying me to keep quiet? The fact that I've been fired but you're paying me £200,000 to go is just an insult. I don't want your money. I just want a chance to explain. But I take it by the fact that you are ghosting me, that you're not going to let me. I will organise the return of the funds, and all the clothes and the gifts you gave me. They remind me too much of what it felt like to be wanted. As angry as I am at you, I wish you and your family all the best.

I hit send and then switched off my phone. I didn't expect a response, but I'd rather not see one if he did send anything.

CHAPTER 13

Justin Feels Betrayed

I sit at my desk in my office, looking at the text I had just received from Jazmin. I didn't think I'd miss anyone this much, but it hurts to read her words.

When I left her flat on Saturday night, I almost turned straight round, but she had lied to me – to all of us – and I couldn't abide liars. The thought of seeing her around the office and not being able to touch her was just too much, so I sorted out a very good redundancy package for her. I had been planning on merging Hammonds into my corporation, so this just gave me the nudge I needed.

I spent the week trying to forget her; the way she smiled whenever she saw me, or the way she enjoyed trying to wind me up. I could still smell her sent on my bedsheets, so I had taken to sleeping in one of the guest bedrooms. That was for the little sleep I got. My dreams were filled with her; how beautiful she looked when she came for me, and the pleasure on her face when she took me in her mouth. "Stop it, Justin!" I shout out loud, "she's just another bit of fun." But she wasn't, and I knew there would never be another like her.

Time would heal these wounds. After I had let myself accept this, I was able to carry on with my work. I had more important things to worry about. It turned out that Andrew has cancer and is not responding well to treatment, and I've got the merger of Hammond Marketing with my company to sort out. Any thoughts of Jazmin needed to stay out of my head so I could focus on what mattered.

The weeks went by slowly, with too many thoughts of Jazmin going through my head. Andrew was getting worse, and I had been trying to find specialist after specialist to try to help. Mum has been giving me grief as well, so I spend my downtime working on one of my bikes. I'm not sleeping, so I might as well.

Chapter 14

What's Next for Jazmin?

It had been over two weeks since I had left Hammonds and the job search was not going well. It was late August, but most of the jobs were still short-term for holiday cover. I had started to think about going into nursing to use my abilities. People with abilities were getting better press these days and it was becoming more accepted.

Emma still wasn't responding to any of my messages, but I had managed to talk to her mum about it all.

"Jazmin, just give her time. You have been friends since you were eight, and she loves you very much. She won't throw that away."

"How can you be so sure? She isn't responding to me at all. I don't even know how things are going for her at The Blake Corporation."

"She's doing fine. She's the PA for the CFO, so a bit of a bump up for her."

"I'm really happy for her. Any chance of letting her know I was asking after her? I don't want to get you stuck in the middle, but I don't know any other way."

"Of course, I can. They are due to come for dinner on Sunday, so I'll have a chat with her then."

"Thank you so much, I really appreciate it."

"That's my pleasure. Now, I'm afraid I'm going to have to love you and leave you as I have a cake in the oven." We said our goodbyes and I promised to come and see them soon. Emma's mum and dad are all I had now.

As I was sorting out my washing that night, I found the note in my pocket from the nurse in A&E who looked after me after I was attacked. Maybe I should give her a ring? It couldn't do me any harm. It was not as though I would lose anything. I took a deep breath and picked up my phone. It rang a couple of times before it was answered.

"Hello?"

"Hello. Is this Nurse Jennings, from St Georges?"

"Who's asking?" the voice said.

"It's Jazmin Cooper. You treated me in A&E, about a month ago."

"Oh yes, I remember – the healer."

"Yes, that's me."

"How can I help?"

"Well, I was wondering how serious you were about the job offer. And if I need any medical training first."

"Yes, oh yes, I was very serious. As you appear to be a very powerful healer, the only training you would need would be to learn all the terminology and the anatomy. So, actually quite a lot, but you can learn on the job. Are you looking for a new job, then?"

"Yes, unfortunately, I find myself jobless, and I can't seem to find anything."

"OK, give me your number and I'll give you a call tomorrow afternoon. I just need to clear it with a few people first, before you start."

"Sorry, does that mean I have a job?"

"Of course, it does. There's no way any hospital would turn you down. We're just lucky you came to us first."

"OK, then, thank you so much. I'll talk to you tomorrow."

I said my goodbyes, thanking her again, and hung up. *Yippee, I've got a job!* Even though Emma wasn't speaking to me, I dropped her a message to let her know. I was not quite sure how she would take it, but at least it might push her to answer. Unfortunately, it didn't – there was no response.

Over the next few days, Nurse Jennings (whose first name was Alice) went through all I needed to know to get me started. I was going to start on one of the wards. It had been agreed that I was to start on first September, so I had a few more days to get prepared. I was booked onto some online classes as well to help start me off. Because they were online, I had already been able to do some of the work, and Alice had been able to change her rota, so she will be my supervisor. At least I would be with someone I knew to start with.

CHAPTER 15

Jazmin's New Job

It was the night before I started my new job, and I wished I could talk to Justin. I'd been really missing him over the last few weeks. I'd been feeling unwell, which was unusual for me. Ever since I had had the illness that put me in hospital, I had not been ill – not even a sniffle.

I had the mobile number for Alice so I dropped her a text:

Hi, Alice, it's Jazmin. I'm a little nervous about tomorrow, so wanted to drop you a line. I hope you don't mind?

That's perfectly fine, don't worry. You're going to do great. I'll meet you outside the hospital just before 7.30am, and I'll take you in.

Thanks, Alice, that's great. I'll see you in the morning.

That night, I dream of Justin. We were in a park, playing catch with a little boy with blue eyes and dark hair, just like Justin's. I woke up with a jolt. It felt so real. I miss him every day. I look at my clock and it was 4am. I had an hour before I needed to get up, but I didn't see me sleeping any more.

I got up and started to get ready. For some reason, I checked my phone, and there was a message from Emma. I opened it immediately. All it said was, "Good luck for today." Not much, but something was better than nothing. "Thank you," I replied. I didn't put any more as I didn't want to push my luck. I continued getting ready and even managed to eat some breakfast.

As I arrived at the hospital Alice was walking towards me from the other direction.

"Morning."

"Morning, Jazmin. You ready?"

"Ready as I'll ever be."

We head in and she takes me straight to HR. I spent the morning with them going through various forms, and then going through what I was expected to do. Alice then took me down to A&E for a few hours, so she could see what I was capable of doing. I sorted out a few bad cuts and fixed a man's broken hand. Not everyone wanted my help but I was OK with that.

We went back up to the ward around 3pm, at which time I took a quick break. They had a staffroom just behind reception, so I sat in there for ten minutes, chatting to one of the nurses. She had been on the ward for four years and loved it.

I eventually finished at 8.15pm, after I had finished helping a patient with heart problems. The joy I felt when they thanked me for what I had done made me glad I had started there.

Over the following weeks I continued with my online training, and helped as many people who would allow me to. I had such a great feeling of achievement. To see these people, who have been so ill, leaving the hospital with a much better outlook, was so heart-warming. Emma and I had started talking again, but she hadn't quite forgiven me yet. I was hoping that by Christmas things would be back to normal. Life was being kind to me. I had even sent a cheque to The Blake Corporation for the majority of the money I had been paid when I had left. I had also returned all the clothes and gifts to Justin, but they came straight back. There was a note that read: *"These were given to you as a gift, I don't want them back. J."* I didn't want anything to do with Justin or The Blake Corporation, so I took all the clothes to a charity shop. At least that way someone else would get some use out of them.

CHAPTER 16

Jazmin's Discovery

It was November, and I was out shopping. My shifts weren't too bad; I would work five days on then three days off. I was on the three-days-off part, so managed to get out. I was walking down one of the aisles in the local pharmacy, when I noticed the sanitary products. That made me think, when did I last have my period? I couldn't remember. *I'm on the pill, so I can't be pregnant. Or can I?*

I grabbed a couple of tests to do when I got home. I tried to carry on with my shopping but I just couldn't focus, so I headed home. Why did this have to happen to me? I got in, dropped my bags on the counter, and grabbed the tests. I headed straight to the bathroom and prayed.

It was the longest two minutes of my life. I tried to potter around the flat; put the shopping away. I just didn't want to know the results, but I knew I needed to look. I didn't really know why I got the tests, my powers gave me the ability to check for myself, but I was too scared. I walked back into the bathroom and took a deep breath. There it was, showing on both of them. Yes, I was pregnant. *Shit, shit, shit.*

I needed to speak to Emma. I grabbed my phone and found her number. I hoped she answered and would talk to me. It rang a couple of times and then she answered.

"Hello?"

"Hi, Emma, it's Jaz. Do you have time for a chat?"

"What's up?"

"Emma, I'm pregnant. And yes, it's Justin's."

"Have you told him yet?"

"I only found out two minutes ago, so no, not yet."

"Are you going to tell him?"

"I don't know. It's all such a shock. We were so careful."

"Oh, honey. What are you going to do? Are you going to keep it?"

"I could never get rid of it. I'm just scared. I'm on my own. I never imagined being a single parent."

"Well, you're not on your own. Shawn and I will help, and so will Mum and Dad."

"Do you really mean that? I know I was wrong to not tell you about my abilities, so I understand if you don't want to get involved."

"Jaz, yes, I am still mad at you for not telling me, but you are my oldest and dearest friend. Of course, I'm going to support you. I'm going to be an aunty. It's so exciting."

"Exciting isn't the word I would use," I say to her. "Thank you so much. I don't feel so alone now."

"So, how far gone are you?"

"I must be about three months."

"You need to go to the doctors so you can be booked in for a scan."

"I'm not even registered with a doctor."

"Then you need to go and get registered. You're going to need various bits for the baby. Also, antenatal classes would be good."

"OK, but hold on, I've only known about this pregnancy for five minutes. I need to get my head around it all."

"OK, I get it. Everything will be OK, and I'll be with you all the way."

"Thank you, Emma, I really appreciate the support. I don't know what I would do without you."

"It's OK, I'm happy to help. Look after yourself, and I'll talk to you soon, but get yourself booked in with a GP."

"Yes, Mum, I will. I'll talk to you soon. 'Bye."

"'Bye," Emma replies.

I felt so much better after my chat with Emma, but the thought of telling Justin scared me. I didn't want anything from him, especially after he fired me, but he did have a right to know. I needed time to think about this.

I knew I was going to keep the baby, so I looked online for a local GP and got myself registered.

I managed to get an appointment for the next day, so I felt I could breathe. I sat down on my sofa and looked around. I might have to move as a studio flat wasn't exactly ideal for bringing up a baby. There was so much to think about and sort out, I just didn't know where to start.

My new doctor was a lovely lady. I explained that I was a healer so I knew that the baby was OK. It was funny how I could hear my baby's heartbeat whenever I wanted. The doctor was happy with everything, and got me booked in for my first scan. I left the surgery, feeling content with how things were going to go. Now I just had to decide when I was going to tell work, and what I was going to do about Justin.

Time moved on and before I knew it, the end of November was in sight. I'd told work about my bump, and most of them were really happy for me.

It was lunchtime and I was sitting in the staffroom eating a sandwich. I had had my first scan a couple of days ago and Emma had joined me. It was wonderful to see my little bundle of joy. Now though I needed to tell Justin, so I sent him a text: *Hi, Justin. It's Jazmin. Sorry to disturb you, but can we meet for a coffee?* I left it at that and sent it. I really didn't know if I wanted to hear from him or not, but he had the right to know that he was going to be a dad.

Alice came up to me and said, "You look like you've just seen a ghost."

"I've just messaged the dad, asking to meet."

"Oh, like that, is it?" she replied.

"I still have feelings for him, but I think I was just a bit of fun to him. So, I don't see the news going down too well. I don't want anything from him, so it's just his right to know."

"Well, there is no point worrying about something you can't control. Anyway, you have a new patient. He has a tumour between his lungs, but he doesn't want the operation to remove it. He's had chemo but it hasn't worked. He is a private patient, so he's been told about the excellent healer we have."

At present, the hospital is only offering my services to private patients. I didn't agree with this, but in the end, I needed the job.

"OK, let me take a look and see if I can help." Now I knew about the pregnancy, I was more careful about how much strain I put on myself, so I could not help everyone completely.

"He came in this morning, so he's in room 11."

"OK, I'll go now." I grabbed his file and walked down the corridor. I knocked and walked in the room just as I was looking at the name. It's Blake, and there's Andrew sat in the bed, with Melanie sitting next to him.

"Andrew, Mel – hi."

"Jazmin! This is a surprise. Where have you been? We haven't seen you in months."

"Didn't Justin tell you? We split up."

"Now I know why he's in such a foul mood all the time. What did my brother do?" Andrew asks weakly.

"It doesn't matter. Now, I believe you would like my assistance?"

"You're the healer?"

"Yes, that would be me, and the reason Justin walked out on me." I say more quietly. "Now, let's take a look at you. If you could pull the bedsheets down. OK. Now, you are going to feel a warming sensation around your chest."

I held my hands out over the affected area and closed my eyes. Warmth radiated around my hands and I could sense the change in Andrew's body. It took me about twenty minutes to get the molecules to act the way I wanted them to, but at least he should start improving over the next few days. "OK, I'm done."

"Already?"

"Yes. It will take a day or two for it to really start to make a difference, but then you should be OK to go home. The doctor will be in later, and will probably want to do a scan and bloods tomorrow to see how it's going."

Melanie got up and walked around the bed. She then gave me a huge hug.

"Thank you so much, Jazmin. You are a miracle worker."

"I'm just happy to help."

"You must come over for dinner one day, especially with Christmas around the corner."

"Thank you for the invite, but I don't think that's a good idea. I don't want to cause any problems between you two and Justin."

"Sod Justin," said Andrew. "You've just saved my life, so he doesn't get a say."

"I don't know. I'll have to see."

"You still have my number, don't you?" asked Mel.

"Yes, it's still in my phone."

"And I have yours. I'll text you some dates, just in case."

"OK. I have to go now. I have other patients to see." I walked out of the room, a little worried. What if Justin turned up to see his brother? They either didn't notice my bump, or they chose not to say anything, but I didn't want Justin to see me and find out about my pregnancy this way. I was almost four months along now, so I was starting to show. I checked my phone – there was no response from my earlier message. I'd give him a couple of days and then try again.

CHAPTER 17

Justin's Reaction

It was August when I last saw Jazmin, and I couldn't believe how much I missed her. The merger of her old company had gone well and I hadn't had to lay off too many people. (One too many actually, but it was too late to change that now.)

Andrew had been taken into hospital today as he was getting worse. I'd been looking into every possible therapy to help him, but I think he had tried them all.

I was sat at my desk in my office when my phone beeped. I picked it up, and I was shocked to see that Jazmin had messaged me, asking to meet. As much as I wanted her in my arms, I couldn't, so I just ignored her.

Just then, Marcus walked in.

"Sir, Miss Cornish is here to see you."

"I don't want to see anyone." Elizabeth Cornish was from a high society family, and I had taken her out for dinner twice. I had no intention of repeating that though after she kept calling me.

"She's saying she won't leave until she speaks to you." Just then, Marcus was pushed out of the way, and a long-legged blonde walked in.

"Justin. There you are."

"Elizabeth, I don't have time right now. Thanks Marcus," and he walked out of my office and closed the door behind him. "What can I do for you, Elizabeth?"

"Oh, Justin, don't be like that," she said as she walked around my desk and stood in front of me. "You know you can't run away from this." Elizabeth pointed between the two of us. "Our families are expecting us to marry. You know that."

"I have no intention of marrying you – not now, not ever."

"Don't be so harsh, baby. Of course, you will. We have that gala dinner tonight for St George's Hospital. You can pick me up at 8pm. And don't be late." She gave me a peck on the cheek and walked out of my office. I had no intention of picking her up any night, so she was going to have a long wait.

"Oh, my god, when will that woman listen?" I said.

"When you are married to someone else," came Marcus's voice.

"You're probably right there. Even then, she may cause problems."

"Just make sure whoever you marry can handle herself." I could think of one woman and one woman only, Jazmin. But she had lied to me, so it couldn't be her.

The day carried on and I got loads done, but I kept thinking about Jazmin, and Marcus's comment about marriage, and that's when I made my decision. I would be getting married, but it wouldn't be to Elizabeth Cornish.

CHAPTER 18

Jazmin's Announcement

It has been two days since I sent the message to Justin, but still no response. I sent another, and an email, just in case something had happened with his phone.

Andrew went back home this morning, looking so much better. The tumour had already shrunk by half, so he should make a full recovery. I even did a sneaky check when he hugged me goodbye. I wanted to make sure one of the Blake men were OK, I couldn't comment on the other one.

It was now the second of December and I still hadn't heard back from Justin. It was starting to really piss me off that he felt so little for me. He couldn't even respond to my messages. I was so pissed that instead of going for lunch with Mel, I cancelled, and found myself outside Justin's building. I was not going to let him ignore me any more. I walked in, and up to the reception desk.

"Is Mr Blake in today?"

"Yes, ma'am, but he's busy."

"That's not a problem," I said, and walked straight past. I got to the lift and luckily one had just arrived. I got in and the doors closed before security could get to me. I knew I wouldn't have long, so I got off the floor before his and sneaked up the stairs.

I could see security waiting for me at the lift, looking confused. *Ha, gotcha.* He had told me about his building, so I knew where to go. I walked along to Justin's' office. The door was closed and I could hear talking behind it.

"No, I don't want anything to do with her." Then a pause. "Why do you think I haven't responded to her?" I stood there not knowing what to think. I tried to tell myself that he was not talking about me, but I still felt the tears well up. I needed to do this so I could move on. I pulled my shoulders back, opened the door, and walked in. At that exact moment, I felt a hand on my shoulder.

"Excuse me, Miss, but you can't go in there."

Somehow, I sent a shock through my body and into the person's arm. I turned as she shouts out:

"Ouch. What was that?"

"You shouldn't stop a woman on a mission."

"Jazmin! Lisa, it's OK, you can let Miss Cooper in. And for future reference, if Miss Cooper comes to this building again, she is to be brought straight to me. Do I make myself clear?"

"Yes, Sir."

"Make sure all relevant staff are informed. I don't want any problems."

"Yes, Sir, I'll do that straightaway. Miss Cooper, would you like a drink?"

"No, thank you, I won't be staying long."

Lisa walked from the office and closed the door behind her. We stood there, just staring at one another. I couldn't help myself. He was still as handsome as he was the last time I saw him. He walked around to my side of the desk and stood in front of me.

"So, what can I do for you, Jazmin?" I snapped myself out of my daze to speak:

"I... I..."

"Yes, Jazmin?"

"I'm sorry for barging in on you like this, but you weren't responding to my messages."

"I know," he said as he stepped closer to me. "I've been a little busy trying to organise something. I was going to come and see you today, but you beat me to it."

"You were?"

"Yes, Jazmin, I was." He was so close to me now that I had to lift my head to be able to look at his face. That very strong jawline and those gorgeous lips... I gave myself another kick and stepped back. I took a deep breath.

"Justin, I came here today to tell you that I'm pregnant as I'm sure you can tell by my bump. And yes, the baby is definitely yours." He went to speak but I held up my hand. "I don't want or expect anything from you, and you don't have to have any involvement. I just thought you had the right to know that you are going to be a Dad."

I stood there for what felt like hours, but was only a matter of minutes. He didn't say anything – not a single thing. He just stood there, looking at me. "Well you know now," and I turned around and walked to the door. As I opened it I turned my head to take one last look at him. Nothing – not a word came from his lips – so I leave.

I got to the lift, pushed the button for the foyer, and waited. I was kind of hoping he would call me back, but he didn't. The lift arrived and I got in. I was desperately trying to hold back my tears, but I could feel them falling. I really thought he would have had something to say, even if it was just to get out. But nothing just hurt so much. I got to the foyer and started walking to the door. I was just about to walk out onto the street, when I heard my name being called.

"Miss Cooper, stop." I continued heading out and grabbed the first taxi I saw. I had no intention of staying in that building any longer, let alone to be told not to come again. He had been so sweet when I arrived, telling his staff to let me in whenever I came to see him. But for him to change so fast, I thought, *I'm better off without him.*

Once I got back to the hospital, I headed to the locker room. I was so upset I just wanted to curl up and cry. I was in tears when Alice walked in and saw me.

"Oh, honey, what's the matter?" she asked.

"Nothing. It doesn't matter," I replied.

"Yes, it does. Now, what's wrong?"

"I went to see the Dad. I told him I was pregnant, and that it was definitely his. I said I didn't expect anything from him, and that's what I got: absolutely nothing. He didn't say anything. Really, I shouldn't be upset. I did say I didn't want anything, but I thought he'd at least tell me to leave, or that I'm a liar. But he just stood there, staring at me. So, I left."

"Oh, honey, I'm so sorry. Just think, you have a beautiful little baby on the way, and friends who are here for you. We will make sure you are OK."

"Thanks, Alice, that's very kind of you to say so."

"My pleasure. Now, get your butt back out there and see your next patient."

"Yes, boss," I said with a smile. I walked out of the locker room, feeling better than I had done going in. It was going to be a tough journey, bringing up 'Bump' on my own, but I knew I could do it. I quickly messaged Emma and told her what had happened, and then got back to work.

It was 8.15pm by the time I walked out of the hospital to head to Emma's. She had invited me to stay over as I was now off for three days. We were almost back to how we were, before I told her about my abilities… almost.

I was standing waiting at the bus stop when a dark-coloured SUV pulled up. I recognised it at once: it was one of Justin's cars. *How does he know where I am? And why on earth is he here?* The door opened, and all I heard was, "Get in."

"No." Luckily just then my bus pulled up so I went to get on. I could hear Justin getting out of the car. I just didn't care any more.

"Jazmin, get in the car, now." I turned around and stared at him.

"I don't work for you any more, Mr Blake. You can't boss me around."

"You're right, you don't, but you are carrying my child, so please get in the car." I stood there for a minute and weighed up my options. If I got on the bus he would just follow me; if I got in the car, I risked getting hurt even more.

"Excuse me, Miss, are you getting on?" I looked at the bus driver, then at Justin.

"It looks like I have a lift, but thank you, anyway." *More hurt it is, then.* I walked away from the bus, towards Justin. "So, why am I getting in this car rather than getting on that bus and heading to Emma's place?"

"Because we need to talk about our future, and our family."

"What?" Now I was confused – our future, and our family? Where had that come from? I got in the car and sat as far away from him as I could. Justin got in and the car pulled into the traffic.

"To my place please, Fred."

"Yes, Sir."

"No," I said. "I'm going to Emma's, so you either take me there or I get out now."

"Fred, you heard the lady."

"Yes, Sir."

"Thank you. Why did you walk out on me earlier?"

"Why didn't you say something?"

"I was in shock. I wasn't expecting you to tell me that I'm going to be a father, and I just froze. I'm sorry, I should have said something."

"Yes, you should have. Like I said, I don't want anything from you; you don't have to be involved. I just wanted you to know." Justin sat there with a smile on his face, his eyes lighting up with a look that I didn't understand or even recognise.

"Oh, I have every intention of being involved, and our child will have everything he or she could possibly want."

"Justin, I don't want our child being spoilt and coming back from yours with loads of gifts. Firstly, I won't have anywhere to put them, and secondly, I want Bump to understand the value of money; how you need to work to get what you want, not have everything given to him or her on a silver platter." Again, Justin just sat there, looking at me with a smile on his face.

"That won't be an issue as there won't be any need to go between two homes."

"You're not taking my baby away from me! Over my dead body! And what's with the smile?" I ask.

"I have no intention of taking our baby away from you. You are going to be a wonderful mother."

"Then what do you mean?" The smile was there again, and it was really starting to annoy me. I was ready to punch him in the face, it annoyed me so much.

"We will be living under the same roof – as a family. We're getting married in a few weeks, and we can either live in my apartment or we can buy somewhere else." It was my turn to sit there, stunned. Who did he think he was, telling me how my life was going to be? Now I was getting angry.

"So, we're getting married and I don't get a say in it? No love, no romance, just we're getting married? Well, you've got another thing coming if you think I'm just going to move Bump and me into your place and marry you. After how you've treated me, you can think again!" Fred had just pulled up outside Emma's place, so I grabbed my bags and got out. Justin jumped out after me.

"Jazmin, you are not raising our child on your own. I want us to be a proper family, so you are moving in with me and we're getting married." The cheek of it! How dare he be like this? I turned around and slapped him hard across the face, thanked Fred for the lift, and walked off. I was fuming. How dare he, after everything I'd been through? This time he followed me, and grabbed me by the arm.

"Please, Jazmin, just think about this for a second. It will be better for the baby if we are together; more stable an environment."

"That's it, is it? You're worried about the environment *my* child will be brought up in? Well, I can tell you now, *my* child will be brought up in a warm and loving environment, with a mother who loves them dearly; not in a house where the father hates their mother because of her abilities." By this stage I was shouting. I turned around and headed for Emma's front door. "And don't you dare follow me." Just as I went to knock, the door flew open and there stood Emma. She looked back and forth between the two of us, and I just say, "Apparently, we're getting married."

"What?"

"Exactly what I said." She moved to the side for me to walk in and then shut the door behind me.

"What was that all about?"

"He turns up at the bus stop and literally drags me to the car. He then apologises for what happened at the office."

"What about the office?"

"I went and told him about Bump today as he hadn't responded to any of my texts or emails. He just froze and didn't say a thing, so I left."

"OK. So, he said sorry for that. What did he say about the baby?"

"Well, that's the marriage bit. He tells me we are going to get married and bring Bump up together. No love, no romance, no proposal – nothing."

"What did you say to that?" Emma asked.

"I said it wasn't happening; that there was no way I was marrying him."

"And?"

"We arrived here. So, you know the rest." Emma sat on her sofa. I could tell she didn't know what to say.

"OK, let me get this straight: you don't see or hear from him in four months and, after a short discussion, he's decided that you're getting married."

"Yep, that's the long and short of it."

"OMG, what's he like? I can't blame you for saying no."

"Oh, Emma, what am I going to do? I want what's best for my baby, but I can't marry someone who doesn't love and respect me. I want my child to see and feel love all around them, and they won't if I marry Justin." I was going to have to think long and hard about what I wanted. I had admitted to myself a while ago that I still loved Justin and that hadn't changed, but as he didn't love me, that made things difficult.

"Your child will feel love and respect because they will have you and me, and Mum and Dad, and even my brother. They will have so much love, they won't know what to do with it. So, for now, let's forget about Mr Billionaire – well yours, anyway – and talk about something else."

"So, how is Shawn?" I asked.

"He's great, but he has seemed a little distant lately, as though he's hiding something."

"I'm sure it's nothing. Christmas is coming up – he probably doesn't know what to get you that you won't moan about."

"Ha-ha, very funny."

"Well, you are a little picky. I always have problems getting you a gift, and I've known you for ever."

"I'm not that bad, am I?"

"You can be sometimes." We both start laughing, and that makes me feel a lot better.

The evening carries on, with Emma slowly getting drunk and me giggling at her.

"So, apart from Shawn seeming a little distant, how are things going with him?"

"Apart from that, they're great. He's asked me to move in with him, so another reason why it's strange how he is behaving at the moment. If you were still with Justin, I'd ask you to ask him." It turned out Shawn and Justin had become good friends since I had last seen him. I suppose, both being billionaires, they had a lot to talk about. Who knows?

"I'm so happy for you, and I would have been more than happy to ask, if things had been different."

"I know. I'm sure things will work out – one way or another."

"I hope so," I said.

"Anyway, I'm tired and need to sleep."

When I eventually got Emma up the stairs and on her bed, I couldn't sleep. All I could think about was my conversation with Justin. Why couldn't he love me and treat me with some respect, just like Shawn did Emma? Life was going so well, and now this.

Over the next few days and weeks, I tried to avoid anything to do with Justin and the baby. I had already received several texts from him, with various suggestions for wedding venues, and mansions up for sale, but it was my turn not to reply.

Chapter 19

Jazmin's New Beginning

It was Christmas Eve, and I had been invited to Emma's parents' house for Christmas. I was working on Boxing Day so I had packed enough clothes to be able to go to work from their place.

As I arrived, the front door flew open and Emma ran out.

"Happy Christmas, Bump."

"Hey, what about me?"

"And to you, too." Emma took my bags and helped me into the house.

Emma's parents lived down the road from her, in a quiet road. It was a Victorian house which had large rooms with high ceilings. It was beautifully decorated and always felt very homely. It had four bedrooms so plenty of room for me to stay over. We went into the main living room where the rest of her family were. She had one younger brother called Richard. He was in the middle of a law degree. His intention was to join his parents' firm, once he had passed.

"Jazmin, you made it."

"Of course, Emily. I wouldn't miss Christmas with you all for all the tea in China. Just next year, you'll have to put up with the little one as well."

"Yes, she'll be about seven months old by then. It will be so wonderful to have a small child around again at Christmas."

"So, you think I'm having a girl, do you?"

"Yes, you are. Well, I think you are." I didn't want to burst her bubble but I knew full well what I was having. Being a healer, I knew what was going on in my own body, and have been chatting quite happily to Thomas. Yes, I was going to have a boy. He seemed to like the name as he squirmed each time I called him that. I couldn't wait to meet him; I just wished things were better with his dad.

I put the presents I had brought with me under the tree, gave everyone big hugs, and then curled up in my normal corner. I always loved Christmas with the Slowne family. They were always so happy, and always included me in everything.

"Dinner will be soon." I went to get up to help. "Oh no you don't, Jazmin. You put your feet up and rest. You'll have plenty of running around to do once my granddaughter arrives." (As you can see, well and truly part of the family.)

"Emily, give her a break. She hasn't even told us if it's a boy or a girl, so stop pushing her."

"Edward, it's just a bit of wishful thinking." As they stood there bickering, the doorbell rang. I looked at Emma and mouthed, *who's that?*

"Our special guest."

"What's going on? What special guest? We never have a special guest."

"Please don't be mad at me, but I spoke to him the other day, and I thought this was a good idea."

"What have you done, Emma?" Emily went to answer the door. When she came back in, none other than Justin was walking behind her.

"Emma," I whisper, "why is he here?"

"Please just give him a chance. You might be pleasantly surprised."

"Mrs Slowne, thank you for the invite." Justin then looked around the room and saw me. He smiled that sexy smile of his. "Where should I put these presents?"

"You shouldn't have brought anything; that's very kind of you. Please put them under the tree with the others." Justin did just that, and then sat down next to me.

"What are you doing here?"

"I was invited – the same as you were." I had been looking forward to this Christmas, but not so much now. Why did Emma have to do this? She has a lot to say for herself.

"Surely you want to be with your family on Christmas Eve?"

"I am," he said as he took my hand. "I'm with you and Bump. We just happen to be at your best friend's parents' house." I pulled my hand away, and he chuckles. "I don't want you here."

"Yes, you do, and you know why?"

"Why?"

"Because you love me, and you want to be with the people you love at Christmas."

"Who said anything about me loving you?"

"Emma did." I stared over at her and she smiled back at me.

"Emma, you and I need to have a little chat."

"Later, after dinner." Just as she said that, Emily came in.

"Dinner is served." We all got up and started to leave the living room. Justin followed close behind me. As we entered the dining room, Emily guided us to our seats.

"Jazmin, if you sit next to Dad, and Justin, you can sit next to Jazmin. Emma and Shawn, please sit the other side. Richard, next to Justin, please". As we all sat down, Justin whispered in my ear:

"This is going to be a great Christmas." I didn't say anything; I didn't even react. I tried to ignore him through the whole meal, but it wasn't easy. He would try to involve me in his conversations with the family, and put his hands on me whenever possible.

"Justin, please stop. This is my one time of the year when I feel I belong. Please don't ruin it for me."

"I'm not here to ruin anything for you; I'm here to make it better."

"How? By making me angry and upset?"

"That's not my intention, I promise you that." I started to help Emily clear the table, and Justin followed.

"Emily, please let me sort all this out. You go and sit down."

"But—"

"Emily, please. I can clear up a few plates and put them in the dishwasher."

"OK. Justin, do you mind helping?"

"Not at all, Emily. And thank you again for a wonderful meal."

"My pleasure," she replied.

"Emily stop flirting with him."

"Sorry, dear. Now, don't be too long – we'll open some presents next." (We always opened a couple of presents on Christmas Eve, then the rest in the morning. I didn't know why; it has just always been that way.)

"We won't be long." Emily left the kitchen, and Justin and I got on with clearing up, or should I say, I cleared up and he watched. "Are you going to help me, or just stare?" I asked.

"I'm enjoying the view, so I might just stay here."

"Why are you doing this? One minute you act as though you can't stand me, and then the next you say things like that. What am I meant to think?" Justin started walking towards me with that cheeky grin on his face again.

"Jazmin, I've been a complete and utter idiot."

"Well, I know that – it's no secret." He reached where I was standing, and took my face in his hands.

"I have never known anyone like you, and it was a real shock to me to have these feelings. When you showed us your abilities, I didn't know what to think." He took my hands and held them tightly. "I felt as though you had lied to me, and I hate liars."

"I didn't lie; I just didn't tell you. We hadn't known each other very long. I hadn't even told Emma, and I've known her since I was eight," I said.

"I know, and I realise that now. Not being around you for the last four months has been hell, but I was too stubborn for my own good. I spoke to Mum and Dad, and they told me what an idiot I was being. They had expected me to marry someone else, but when they realised how much you meant to me, they were telling me to not let you go. The day you came to my office I was planning on coming to see you and ask your forgiveness, but you came and told me about our child. When you left, I decided that there was no way I was letting you go."

"But that was three weeks ago, Justin. What have you been doing for the last three weeks?"

"I know, but I had to put plans in place. Obviously, some of them didn't work, as telling you we were getting married was too much."

"So, what now?" I asked.

"Now I tell you the truth: I love you. I have loved you from the moment I met you. You are so strong, and those eyes of yours are so captivating. You are kind and supportive, even with everything you've been through. How could anyone not love you?" I found myself crying; I was so surprised with what he was saying to me.

"Really? You love me?"

"With all my heart and soul, and I intend to spend the rest of my life showing you."

"But what about my abilities, and the fact that I didn't tell you?"

"Your abilities are a godsend. Andrew told me what you did for him, and there is no way our family can ever repay you. I was a fool to walk out on you that day and I have regretted it ever since. I've just been far too stubborn to come and see you until now. Can you ever forgive me for how I have been?"

"Justin, Justin, Justin – what am I going to do with you?"

"Forgive me, I hope, plus a few other things, if I'm lucky."

"Justin, now is not the time."

"Sorry, my love. So, do you forgive me?"

"Please forgive him so we can get to unwrapping some presents." I turn around and find my adoptive family all standing in the doorway.

"How long have you all been there?"

"Long enough to know that he is really sorry, and you should kiss and make up already."

"Then maybe you should all leave, so I can make up my mind."

"OK, we'll go, but hurry up." Once they had left I turned back to Justin.

"If you every do anything like that to me again, you know I will be out that door faster than an F1 car."

"You like F1? I'll take you to some of the races."

"Stop changing the subject."

"Sorry. No, I will never do it again, I promise. I will always pay attention, and always put you and Bump first. I love you, and I can't lose you again." That was all I needed to hear. I threw myself at him and held him tight. I then found his lips and showed him how much I loved him, our tongues caressing one another's, familiarising ourselves once again. When we broke apart, I said:

"Justin, I love you too, so much."

We finished putting the bits in the dishwasher and the condiments away, and headed back to the living room, hand in hand. I went to sit next to him but he pulled me onto his lap. This time I didn't mind. I knew he loved me and I loved him. "Oh."

"What?"

"The baby just kicked." Justin put his hand on my tummy and held it there.

"Jesus, he can kick."

"Who said it's going to be a boy?" said Emily. "I think she's having a girl, but I have a feeling Jazmin knows and just isn't telly anyone." I just chuckled.

"We will all find out when Bump is born in May."

"That's not fair," said Emma.

"When you have your own children, you can play the guessing game with us all." Emma put her hands up in surrender.

"OK, OK, I get the message. But I can promise you, I will. And no cheating from you with your powers, missy." She points to me, as she says this.

"Hey, you're not even pregnant and you're having a go. Give me a break."

"Well, I can sort that out," said Shawn, and we all laughed. I smiled at Emma and got up off Justin's lap.

"Time for a little present."

The evening went on, with stories being told and a game of cards. Justin and I sat in our corner chatting about the baby.

"Would you consider moving in with me? You don't have to answer now, just think about it, please."

"Yes, I'll think about it. I will need to move at some point as I can't bring up a child in a studio flat."

"Just remember, you're not on your own. I can't wait to be a dad, and I will be the best dad I can possibly be. That said, I also intend to spoil you rotten. Now, if you don't want to move in with me, at least let me help you with a new apartment. There are a couple of places in my building. At least I would be nearby, if you need me."

"I probably wouldn't be able to afford any of the places in your building, but thank you for the offer."

"Hey, there are perks to dating the landlord, you know."

"Oh really?"

"Yes. It means you pay very low, if not non-existent, rent."

"I couldn't live there without paying my way, Justin, I just wouldn't feel right. I'm used to paying my way."

"I know, but I earn more in an hour than you probably do in a year. "So, how's it going at St George's?"

"It's great. I'm really enjoying it. I'm also studying nursing online."

"When do you have time for that?"

"It's usually late-night studying, after a long shift."

"You're doing too much; you need to stop. You're risking your health, and our baby's." Justin didn't look happy about my workload, but he needed to understand that I was in a better position than anyone to know the health of myself and our baby. I turned around on Justin's lap and looked him straight in the eye.

"Justin, please believe me when I say that I can categorically promise you that both myself and our baby are 100 per cent OK. I will know before any midwife or doctor if something goes wrong, so stop worrying and enjoy Christmas."

"So, what are you doing for Christmas day?" I asked Justin.

"Here with you – if that's OK?" he replied.

"You'll need to check with Emily and Edward."

"I already have. My bag is in my car."

"Have you been conspiring behind my back?"

"My love, if it means I get to be with you I will conspire with whomever I need to." I gave him a light punch to the chest and smirked.

As we were all sitting curled up, chatting, Shawn suddenly got up. He was looking very nervous as if there was something very important he wanted to say. He turned to Emma and spoke.

"Emma, ever since we met, you have been the light of my life. You are everything a man could ever want. You keep me in check, with your wit and quick retorts, and are always there when I need support." Shawn got down on one knee. "Emma Louise Slowne, love of my life, will you do me the great honour of becoming my wife?" He pulled out a ring box from his pocket and opened it up. Emma was sitting there with her mouth wide open, and the rest of us were on the edge of our seats, waiting to see what she would say. She looked over at me and I nodded. Shawn has been so good to her, she would be a fool to say no. She turned to Shawn.

"Well," she said, and paused.

"Don't leave him kneeling there – give him an answer," said Edward. She smiled.

"Yes, Shawn, I will marry you." He put the ring on her finger, and we all jumped up. Justin suddenly produced some rather expensive-looking champagne.

"Did you know about this?"

"Shawn and I may have had a few conversations." Once Emma's parents and brother had said their congratulations and given the couple lots of hugs and kisses, it was my turn.

"I'm so happy for you both."

"Thank you," Emma said. "Just make sure you say yes to your man when he asks." Shawn leans in.

"He loves you very much."

"And he knows he fucked up," said Emma.

"I'm aware of that, but it doesn't mean I'd say yes just yet. Anyway, let's see the ring." It was a beautiful pink diamond with little white diamonds around it. It was stunning, and reflected the Christmas lights all around the room. It was as though rainbows were dancing on all the surfaces. It was beautiful. I then noticed Shawn giving someone a bit of a strange headshake.

"Excuse me, ladies." Shawn walked away, and I saw him go to Justin.

"Justin, I'm not sure if this is the right time to be asking her. It might be too soon. She obviously loves you very much, but she's guarding herself. I may be wrong, but I thought I should let you know," Shawn said to Justin.

"Thanks, mate, I appreciate what you're saying, but I think I will try, anyway."

I scrunched up my forehead and turned back to Emma.

"What's going on there?"

"I don't know," she said. "Oh well, we'll leave them to it. Let's celebrate."

"Yippee, I get to celebrate with orange juice – what fun."

"It's not for too much longer, and you'll have a beautiful little baby to cuddle."

"I know, it just would have been nice to be able to celebrate this properly with you." Justin then came over.

"Come here, baby, and give me a hug." I put my arms around his waist and held him tight.

"What's the matter?"

"Nothing, I just wanted to hold you. It's been too long since I last did."

"It's been all of about ten minutes."

"Yes, ten minutes too long." I laughed.

"You're silly."

"Yes, silly and in love."

"Come on, let's go and sit back down." Justin followed behind and we sat back on the sofa. The conversation turned to weddings and all the preparation needed. Shawn was saying that Emma could have whatever she wanted.

"I have to say, I wouldn't want such a big fuss; just a quiet ceremony with the people here and maybe a couple of friends from the hospital," I whispered to Justin.

"You can have whatever you want. You've just got to say yes to marrying me, first."

"Why? Are you asking?"

"Why? Would you say yes if I did?"

"I might do. I don't know."

"Then I'm not asking yet." When he said that, I actually felt quite disappointed. I was surprised as I thought it was too soon; we only just got back together a few hours ago. Bump was kicking around as well, as if he was trying to tell me something. I sat there on the sofa, with the man I love, while he played with my fingers, mainly my ring finger.

"What are you doing?"

"Just checking something," he said. "Yes, I think it will fit."

"What are you talking about?" He looked into my eyes and produced a small box.

"This." He then whispered to me: "Jazmin Isabel Cooper, ever since I met you, you have kept me on my toes. You have challenged me and surprised me, more than any other person alive. You have shown me what it is to love and to be loved in return. I couldn't imagine my life without you. Will you do me the utmost honour of becoming my wife?" I looked around the room and saw Emma smiling at me. She gave me a nod, just the same way I had done to her.

"Yes, Justin, with all my heart, yes." Justin slid the ring onto my finger. He took me in his arms and kissed me. He poured all his love into that kiss, and I knew everything was going to be OK.

"So, we have a double celebration, then," said Edward. "Just no champagne for you, Jazmin."

"I can have a small glass."

"That's not what you said a short while ago."

"A short while ago, it was only Emma getting married; now it's both of us." Corks start popping around us as Emma and I compare rings. Shawn was the CEO of his own technology company so he wasn't shy of a penny or two, either. My ring had a blue, teardrop diamond in the centre, with smaller diamonds around the band. It was exquisite. It was my turn to get congratulated as the family gathered around Justin and myself. I was so happy.

We all sat down, chatting and drinking champagne (well, not so much the drinking for me). I didn't think I could be any happier.

"Justin, how did you know that Shawn was going to propose to Emma today?" I whispered in his ear.

"I bumped into him at Tiffany's when I was ordering your ring. That's when we came up with the plan, and spoke to Emily and Edward about it. They were more than happy to help, especially as both Shawn and I asked for their permission. So, fancy getting married tomorrow?"

"Justin, that doesn't give me any time. Can't we wait until after the baby is born?"

"Whatever you want is fine by me."

CHAPTER 20

Jazmin's Home

I moved in with Justin on New Year's Eve. We had both families over, and had a wonderful time. It was one of the best Christmas and New Year's I had ever had.

I carried on working at the hospital until my due date as I knew Thomas would be late. Justin wasn't particularly happy about it, but there wasn't a lot he could do, unless he locked me in our apartment. I couldn't have been happier.

Compared with how my life had started, and the problems I had had with my parents, I was now a parent myself, and determined to ensure that our child knew he was loved, always.

We married on my birthday. Justin wanted me to have better memories of that day, rather than of my parent's death and Emma walking out on me. The ceremony was simple, and held on a beach in Hawaii. We stayed there for our honeymoon, but not for too long, as we wanted to get back to Thomas. He had been born 3 months before.

It was an amazing place, with clear blue skies and beautiful turquoise waters. I could have stayed there for ever. We spent our days lazing around on our private beach, and our nights enjoying each other's bodies. (Well, for some of it anyway. There was a little incident, but that's for another time.)

"Morning, my beautiful wife. How are you feeling on this fine, sunny morning? "I'm doing good thanks."

"Well, I'm taking you home today so get that beautiful butt of yours out of bed and in the shower."

"Only if you join me," I said.

"If I join you, we will never leave, and I want you home – safe."

"OK, my dear husband. I will have a very lonely shower, then." I jumped out of bed and headed straight for the shower. I really wanted to get home to see Thomas, who had been with Emma while we'd been here.

Within a couple of hours, we were in our private jet, and heading home to start our new lives as a married couple, and family of three.

Epilogue

"Thomas Edward Blake, what are you doing?"

"Mummy, I love you."

"I love you too, sweetie. Now, where is your daddy?"

"Daddy in the garden."

We had moved into a spacious and beautiful house near to Emma and her family once we had got back from our honeymoon. It had a lovely garden, and Justin enjoyed tinkering with his bike while sitting there with the wildlife around him.

"Do you think you can go and get him? Tell him that I can sense that our guests are almost here."

"OK, Mummy."

It was Thomas's third birthday, and all the family were coming to celebrate. I was seven months' pregnant with our second child and Emma was pregnant with their first. We were due around the same time, so had each other for support. I couldn't wait to meet our little girl. It was Justin's turn to choose the name but he wasn't saying what it was. It was a little frustrating!

Thomas ran back into the kitchen.

"Mummy, Daddy is coming."

"Thank you, Thomas. Can you help Mummy and put your top back on, please?"

"Don't want to."

"Come on, Son, do as your Mother asks."

"OK, Daddy."

Justin walked into the kitchen and came up behind me, putting his arms around me, with his hands on my bump.

"How is Bump doing?"

"She's doing fine. She wants to know her name," I said to Justin.

"Nice try, but I'm not telling you."

"What if she doesn't like it?"

"She will because her Daddy chose it for her."

Thomas suddenly screamed and ran to me. "Mummy, my finger – it's bleeding." "What have you done now?" He showed me his hand, and there was a scratch about a centimetre long on his left palm.

"Mummy fix."

"Yes, Mummy will fix."

It turned out that being able to heal any living thing wasn't my only ability – something we learned on our honeymoon. But that was another story...

The End